I0733235

# Honeymoon for Three

# CHRIS KENISTON

Indie House Publishing

# BOOKS BY CHRIS KENISTON

***Hart Land***
Heather
Lily
Violet
Iris
Hyacinth
Rose
Calytrix
Zinnia
Poppy

***Farraday Country***
Adam
Brooks
Connor
Declan
Ethan
Finn
Grace
Hannah
Ian
Jamison
Keeping Eileen
Loving Chloe
Morgan

***Aloha Series Heartwarming Edition:***
Aloha Texas
Almost Paradise
Mai Tai Marriage
Dive Into You
Look of Love
Love by Design
Love Walks In

Shell Game
Flirting with Paradise

***Surf's Up Flirts:***
**(Aloha Series Companions)**
Shall We Dance
Love on Tap
Head Over Heels
Perfect Match
Just One Kiss
It Had to Be You

**Honeymoon Series**
Honeymoon for One
Honeymoon for Three
Honeymoon for Four

***Other Books***
**By Chris Keniston**

**Family Secrets Novels:**
Champagne Sisterhood
The Homecoming
Hope's Corner

# CHAPTER ONE

When Pam Stuart, formerly Baker, formerly Amadeo, formerly—and briefly—Harris, nee Watson's fiancé Leo suggested a destination wedding, she knew this could be her one shot at romance on a cruise ship.

"What about this?" Angie Cannon, Pam's maid of honor, held up a frilly knee length nightie with capped sleeves, faux fur edges, and too many layers of fabric.

"Ange. I'm not a rock star. All I need is something that can be taken off more easily than it can be put on. And *that* doesn't fit the bill." What Pam really needed was something that made her look ten years younger, not like an over-aged Barbie doll.

Angie cocked a single brow higher than the other. "If you're in such an all fired hurry to take it off I don't see why you bother wearing anything at all."

"Surely by now you've learned that for a man it's all about the chase, even after the I Do's. There has to be at least a little mystery right up to the last second."

"Right. Mystery." Angie rolled her eyes and held out a simple spaghetti strap sheer negligee with swaths of heavier fabric in all the right places. "And this?"

Pam bobbed her head and smiled. "Now you're getting the idea." She added the garment to the growing stack of cruise clothes. The first time she'd married had been for love. At least the closest thing possible to forever love at the ripe old age of eighteen. Each wedding after that had probably leaned more toward hopeful than love, but she'd given each husband her best effort. This time she'd smartened up and done things the old fashioned way.

Instead of expecting fireworks and crashing waves, she went for stability, compatibility, and Leo's hefty bank account went a long way toward lifetime security.

Not that he wasn't a nice guy. He was. Very nice. Friendly, funny, charming, not bad looking and a pretty good kisser too. Plus, it certainly worked in her favor that he was royally ticked off at his recent ex trophy wife and looking for a lifetime companion closer to his own age. Pam might not be that close to his age, but she wasn't young enough to be his daughter either and that had counted for something. Her future husband had learned the hard way that reliving his twenties wasn't all it was cracked up to be. Pam wasn't all that sure her twenties had been worth it the first time around.

"I think this about does it." Pam made an awkward effort to raise her garment laden arm. "I can't believe we sail in less than a week."

"I wish it were tomorrow. I am so ready for a little rest and relaxation." Angie beamed. "And maybe a few of those famous Bailey's Banana Coladas Michelle loves so much."

"Now you're talking." Pam laughed at her friend's silly grin. If not for the absurd twist in Pam's former co-worker's wedding plans, Angie and Pam might never have even met. Now Pam couldn't imagine a better best friend. "And who knows, maybe you'll meet the love of your life on board, like Michelle did."

"Fat chance." Angie shook her head. "It will be nice to see her and Kirk again. It's been a while. I just wish they were bringing the baby."

"I can't blame them for leaving her home. I'm sorry Corrie can't come either; that kid sister of Michelle's is growing up nicely. But I think staying home with the baby and letting Michelle and Kirk have a nice vacation is a smart move." Pam's cell sounded off. A sudden jolt zipped through her at the familiar area code. It had been years since she'd spoken with anyone from her hometown. Not since the day she's gone home to bury her father had she set foot in that sorry place, and even then all the old nags had nothing better to do but carry on over ancient history. No.

Whoever had the urge to kick up the past was going to have to find someone new to jaw with. She'd heard enough about her sudden marriage and even faster divorce during her last days in Podunk Georgia, no need to listen to any more of it now.

"Who is it?"

"No idea." She rejected the call, sucked in a deep breath, and tossed off the sour memories. Not that the brief marriage had been distasteful, she'd loved Gil and being Mrs. Pamela Harris. But the price of staying married would have been too high—for Gil. "Let's stop at the Bun Shack. I'm feeling a craving for a smothered in onions swiss cheese burger with all the trimmings."

The phone sounded off again, same number. What the heck could they want?

"Sounds like someone really wants to reach you."

And Pam was just curious enough now to want to know why. "Hello."

"Pammy? Is this still your number?"

No one called her Pammy any more. "This is Pam."

"Oh, good. This is Marjorie Lane. I still have your number from when your daddy was sick."

The old lady had been good to Pam's father in those last months. No matter how much of a gossip the old bird was, Pam couldn't bring herself to be rude. "Nice to hear from you, Mrs. Lane."

"Listen, Pammy, it's none of my business but there's been a lot of talk about town."

Oh brother, now what? After all these years, weren't these people tired of talking?

"Seems some fancy law firm from Chicago's been poking their nose around at the county courthouse. Eloise Hannigan says they were wanting records." She paused for one very long moment and Pam wondered if the line had gone dead. Or maybe the old broad had. "The records they wanted were 'bout you. I didn't let on that I might know how to reach you, but I thought I owed it to your Daddy to give you a heads up. You know, for old time's sake. Just in case. Whatever it is, if there's a lawyer involved, it can't be good."

"Thank you, Mrs. Lane. I appreciate the call, but it's probably just a scam. Some prince from Nairobi wants to leave me all his money."

"Well, just the same—"

"I'm sure it's nothing." Pam reminded herself the old gal had been her father's only friend for years after her mother had passed away. "Thanks again."

"Very well. Now that I know this is still your number, I'll let you know if I hear anything more. Take care, dear."

Before Pam could repeat there was nothing to worry about the call had been cut off and she was left with a chill deep in her bones. The last thing she wanted now—so close to her wedding—was a blast from her past.

For Gil Harris there were a lot of good reasons for getting married. Things he was looking forward to. This morning's den of scowling attorneys was not one of them.

"There appears to be a small discrepancy in the current data."

The last time the lawyers had mentioned anything small, it had taken a stack of papers and hours of conversation to resolve. Not for him and Karen, they had no problem with any of the arrangements. But Karen's father was another story. The man had presented Gil with reams of papers to sign before the wedding less than a month away. Today's prenup was to be the last mountain for him to climb. He counted to ten before asking the obvious question, "What's the discrepancy?"

"Your marital status."

"What about it? I'm single."

"No." The lead attorney in the required dark blue suit with the red power tie shook his head.

"Okay, divorced. Same thing for all intents and purposes."

This time all three lawyers shook their heads at him. The uneasy feeling in the pit of his stomach told him this was no joke.

"It seems," the attorney on the left who bore a striking resemblance to the Pillsbury Dough Boy shoved a paper across the conference table, "all is not as you presented."

Gil glanced at the paper in front of him. A copy of his marriage license to Pam. They'd been married all of a few weeks before things began to unravel. When he glanced up, another paper was shoved in front of him. The divorce papers he'd reluctantly signed. The same ones he'd given Karen's attorneys along with his bank statements, tax returns, and blood type. "What is this all about?"

"There's only one signature on the divorce papers."

"That's because that's my copy. The one filed with the courts should have Pam's signature as well." Gil resisted rolling his eyes. He didn't have time for this. "Gentlemen, just give me the final draft of the prenup so Karen and I can move on to the business of getting married."

"And there lies the problem. No county in Georgia has any record of your divorce. You can't marry Karen." Three heads shook and Gil's stomach did a rather clumsy somersault. "Like it or not, you and Pamela Watson are still legally married."

# CHAPTER TWO

Who would have thought in this day and age of big brother watching and internet tracking that finding one feisty redheaded ex-wife would have been so blasted hard.

"The report is quite thorough considering the short time frame you gave us." After two days of surfing the net searching for a Pamela Elizabeth Watson, Gil finally had to give up and hire a private detective.

At first he'd casually flipped through the multiple pages the PI had provided, quickly scanning the information. Now he was looking more carefully at the details. Pam hadn't had any better luck at picking a husband the second time around. Nor the time after that. Tiny pins pricked at his heart. He'd hoped all this time that she'd found someone to make her as happy as they'd been those first few weeks before everything changed.

Sucking in a deep breath, he set the pages aside. "You're sure this is the right Pam Watson?"

The lanky man across the desk gave a single dip of his chin. "There's a photograph in the envelope."

Photograph? Gil reached for the manila envelope the report had come in and tilted it upside down. A single picture drifted out. The proof of identity he'd asked for. Immediately his gaze fell on the array of colors staring up at him. Pam had always liked bright hues. He'd have thought with time she'd have outgrown her fashion choices, but according to this photo she seemed to have developed quite a flair for standing out.

A smile tugged at one side of his mouth. He'd never known what to expect when he was with Pam, and something told him that would still hold true today. Carefully fingering the edge of the glossy eight by ten, Gil studied it a bit more. A few years older, as was he, but she still looked awfully good. Her eyes held that same twinkle that would have everyone in the room wondering what she knew that they didn't. And her figure was just as slender yet curvy. According to the report, none of her marriages had produced children.

"Thank you very much." He pushed away from his seat and stood. "I'll take it from here."

The PI extended his hand. "Let us know if you need anything else."

Gil remained on his feet until the detective had closed the office door behind him, then slowly he eased back into his seat. Most of the folks back home had gossiped left and right about what had prompted the hasty marriage and almost immediate divorce. The blame always falling squarely on Pam, and she hadn't deserved any of it. Small towns could be vicious against their own. He couldn't blame Pam for moving far away from nowhere Georgia as soon as she could.

By the time he graduated college he hardly ever wanted to go back to that narrow-minded town either. With a master's degree under his belt and a successful career, making time for visiting Porterville, Georgia was no where on his agenda. It was simply easier for his parents to come to him. And now with a pack of nieces and nephews scattered across the countryside, family gatherings were few and far between. Maybe this year, he and Karen would make the time to go to his sister Tammy's for Thanksgiving. It would be the first time in years the entire family would be together, and something about digging through his past in search of Pam had him missing his family more than he'd ever allowed himself to before.

Now he faced a new dilemma. Should he simply pick up the phone and call Pam? There was no time for snail mail. And even if there were, though a lot of years had passed, he didn't want to send a cold, impersonal letter. Setting the photo down with a sigh, he reached for his cell phone. Not the best way to relay complicated news, but there wasn't time for much more.

The truth was he probably wanted to hear her voice a little too much for his own good. Carefully punching in the number highlighted on the first page of the report, Gil sat back in his chair and waited for the call to go through. At the first ring his stomach clenched and he sucked in a deep breath, forcing himself to relax. The second ring sounded and he blew out the breath. The third ring was cut short with a snippy, "Hello."

He didn't need to be an FBI profiler to recognize the woman answering the phone was not pleased with his interruption. She probably thought he was a sales call. "Pam?"

Silence on the other end hung a tad longer than he would have expected. About to announce himself and hope she didn't hang up on him, a softer, weaker voice, responded. "Ye...es?"

There was no way he should be able to recognize her voice on a single, elongated syllable, but nonetheless the brief throaty sound sent his mind whirling back too many years. "Pam, this is Gil. Gil Harris."

Another long pause had him squirming in his seat, wondering if maybe he should have just let the PIs handle this.

"Hi, Gil."

"You sound good." A dumb thing to say, but it was the truth.

Pam let out a nervous laugh. "You can tell that from two words?"

"Yeah," he relaxed, "I can."

"How are you doing?" Her voice came across less stressed, more like what he remembered. Almost as if she cared.

"I'm good. Getting married in a few weeks." No sense in beating around the bush.

"Oh." Slightly higher pitched again, he could once again hear the strained effort in her voice. "That's...nice."

"Which is why I'm calling—"

"To tell me you're getting married?" This time her tone took on the attitude of a wise cracking New Yorker. Not that she'd ever lived in New York. At least the report hadn't said so.

"Well, yes and no," he answered. And just like that he knew this was not something he could just blurt out on the phone, but that didn't help him with what to say next.

"Listen," the single word dripped with impatience, "it's really nice of you to call and reconnect and all. Really. But I'm running around like a chicken with her head cut off. I've got my maid of honor sifting through what suitcase to borrow, two weeks of clothes to narrow down to under fifty pounds worth of luggage without wrinkling the wedding dress, and a fiancé who doesn't understand why I don't have time to see him tonight. Especially if he expects me to get to the port in Miami in time to sail on the *Atlantis* tomorrow. Maybe we can touch base and catch up when I get back."

"You're getting married *again*?" The second his mouth snapped shut, Gil knew he'd made a mistake. If only he could rewind and substitute some other more appropriate comment, like congratulations or best wishes or just about anything else. He didn't have to have spent the last years with Pam to know his tone and choice of words sounded like a judgmental jerk instead of a startled *legal* husband. "I mean—"

"Don't bother. I really don't have time. Let's just say it's been nice and call it a day. I have to go. And congrats on your impending nuptials. Whoever she is, I'm sure she's a lucky girl."

"No—" the call disconnected. "You don't understand," he mumbled into thin air.

Now what? He stared at his phone. Call back? Oh yeah, that would accomplish a lot. Really tick her off so she hangs up on him—again. If she answered at all? Besides there was a bigger problem now than just his impending nuptials. If he turned this over to the PIs to deal with, they might not reach her before the wedding. Letting her commit bigamy was not an option. At least not now that he knew better. Not to mention he had no idea what kind of man she was marrying and if he'd understand the snafu. So where the heck did that leave him?

*Atlantis*. Port of Miami. Setting his phone on the desk he reached for the keyboard. A few strokes and he had all the information he needed. The *Atlantis* sailed tomorrow at five pm for a two week cruise. Nice. But he had to find a way to fix this fast. All he needed was a few minutes to explain and have her tell him in what county and state she filed the final papers. At least he hoped it would turn out to be that easy. The alternative wasn't going to be fun.

A little more searching and he concluded there were only three or four flights she could possibly be on and still make the sailing. If he caught the first morning flight out of Chicago that would get him to Miami in time to catch her before she left the airport for the port, get his answers, and be back home before Karen even noticed he was gone. At least he certainly hoped so. Otherwise he was going to have two very unhappy women on his hands.

On the deck ready to wave Miami goodbye, Pam watched the crowds still boarding the ship.

"Is Leo on board yet?" Angie asked, her nose to the air, sucking up the Florida sunshine.

"From the minute they let the new passengers on the boat. You know him, always first in line. He's already settled in the suite."

"I think it's kinda sweet that you're not sharing a cabin until after the wedding in St. Marteen. Sort of romantic."

That was the plan. "Figured this time if I'm going for old fashioned, I'm going to do everything right. Besides, I think it's getting Leo all fired up, and that will be fun."

Angie's phone clinked. "Oh, Michelle and Kirk just checked into their rooms. They're going to grab lunch upstairs. They want to know if we'd like to join them."

Pam would rather watch the crowds and bask a short

while longer in the Miami heat. She certainly understood why folks migrated south. She'd love to move into a cabin on a cruise ship and just keep sailing. "You can't be hungry."

"No, not really." Angie leaned more heavily on the railing. "It's still early by my clock."

"The two six-inch Subway sandwiches you scarfed down at the airport probably didn't hurt any."

Biting back a sweet smile, Angie shrugged. "I didn't have time for breakfast before we left the house."

A couple of guys leaned over the railing beside Pam. Not bad looking, the question of course was whether they were here together or *together*. Not that it mattered, she was off the market. But Angie could use a little fun in her life. She was too young to be cloistered at home working late hours almost every day of the week. The few times Pam could drag her out of the house it was only for dinner or a movie. Her friend hardly every joined her at the nightspots for a drink or dancing. Pam really hoped this cruise would loosen her up at bit.

"Looks like we're going to have great weather," the taller fellow with the sandy blonde hair said in her direction.

"Is there such a thing as bad weather in Florida?" Pam tilted her head, studying the two men.

"Depends on whether or not you like rain." The blonde stuck his hand out. "I'm Brian Reynolds, this here is my brother Taylor."

"Nice to meet you." She extended her hand as well. "I'm Pam, and this is my friend Angie."

"You ladies traveling alone?" Taylor asked, as though deciding this talking to strangers wasn't such a bad idea.

"There are a few more friends joining us. This is my wedding cruise."

"Congratulations." For a split second she thought she saw a flicker of disappointment in Blondie's eyes, but that couldn't be, she had a few good years on him. "Great venue for a wedding."

"Angie is my maid of honor. My fiancé's brother is standing up for him. He brought his wife and two kids. My best friend and her husband are joining us from California. Small and intimate." Pam noticed Taylor glancing at Angie. Maybe this cruise thing could work out for Angie after all. "Just the seven of us and the kids."

"They're not really kids. They're in college." Angie added, oblivious to Taylor's interest.

"Sounds like fun just the same." Blondie's smile seemed genuine.

Another place and time and getting to know Blondie better would have been appealing. But not any more. Pam was settling down for real this time. Her cell phone sounded off and she didn't bother to look at the caller ID. "Must be Michelle wanting to convince us to go eat, like there's not going to be food twenty-four seven for the next two weeks. Hello."

"Pam."

One syllable and she knew the voice. After all these years how could one word from one man still make her toes tingle. She stepped away from Angie, turning her back to the now chatting new friends. "Gil, I thought we agreed that there was nothing to say."

"Actually, we didn't. There's something very important for me to say to you. But I'd rather do it in person. Are you still here at the airport?"

Pam glanced around. What did he mean by *here*? "No. I told you. I'm sailing on my wedding cruise." She took two more steps away. "Listen, Gil. I'm flattered you want to visit. But this is simply not a good time. I really have to go."

"Don't hang up! Please."

She almost did exactly that, but something almost desperate in his tone stopped her.

"Pam, I need to know where you filed the divorce papers. What county?"

"Where did *I* file the papers?"

"That's what I said."

"I didn't file anything. I signed the papers my lawyer gave me. His assistant told me that after you signed your lawyer would file. Ask him where he did it."

The acid churning in Gil's stomach for the last couple of hours as it finally dawned on him that he'd missed Pam at the airport was now on fire. Someone somewhere had things back asswards. The way he remembered the situation going down was that he signed a copy, and his attorney was giving it to Pam's attorney for her to sign, and then she and her attorney were to file the papers. He never saw anything with her signature on it. "Pam, are you sure?"

"What do you mean, am I sure? I sat in the lawyer's office. Signed on the dotted line and left."

Slinging his carryon bag over his shoulder, he bypassed the baggage claim area and headed toward the taxi stand area. "This is really important, Pam." He had to take a deep breath himself to stay calm. "Was my signature on those papers?"

"I'm not a senile old lady, Gil. I don't have to think hard. I remember that day like it was yesterday. It's not the same as an ordinary day of going to the grocery store for milk and bread. Things like signing divorce papers have a way of sticking with you. Mr. Henry's legal assistant pulled the pages off the printer, set them in front of me and showed me where to sign. Mine was the only signature."

Gil stopped walking. Pinching the bridge of his nose he couldn't think of any way that would be a good way to say this. "I want you to stay calm, but if what you say is correct, and I have no reason to doubt you, then there's trouble in paradise."

"What kind of trouble?" The hint of anger in her earlier tone slipped away giving in to a nervous crack.

"Pam, we're still married."

# CHAPTER THREE

Securing passage on the ship at the last minute was only the beginning of Gil's mad dash to make things right. With nothing but an overnight case, he had some fast shopping to do. And with only a couple of hours until the ship sailed, he couldn't afford to be fussy. A speedy run through Walmart on the way to the ship was his best option. The cabdriver was more than happy to leave the meter running while he shopped. Thank heavens there was no chance of him running into anyone he knew.

Except for Pam. For some strange reason he didn't want her to see him dressed in Wal-Mart specials like the kid she'd married, he wanted her to see what he'd made of himself. The man he'd become. But what difference did it make. This wasn't about them, this was about a divorce.

A Destination Divorce. Why not? The ship had to have internet, and his lawyers were about to earn their retainer. By the time the *Atlantis* docked at the next port he hoped to have all the problems corrected. Pam could have her destination wedding and he'd make it back to Chicago for the elaborate affair Karen's family had orchestrated. If not, he'd rather live on grape leaves on a deserted island than confirm to Buchanan, Buchanan, and Foster Attorneys at Law the fiasco of his marital status.

Earlier in the cab he'd put an emergency call into his lawyer. The man had the nerve to be in court earning a living. Tossing his purchases into the suitcase, Gil made a point to leave the tags in the plastic bags. Just as the taxi pulled up to the passenger drop off area, Gil's phone rang. Bluetooth in his ear, he handed the cabbie his fare along with a handsome tip, and quickly explained the mess to his lawyer. "I don't know who screwed this up, but you've got two days until we make the next port to figure out what actually went down and how to fix it."

"That shouldn't be a problem. Find out where and when your ex-wife's wedding is scheduled and with a little luck there will be a quickie island divorce port before it."

"I want it done right this time, Stewart. I do not want to deal with Larry, Curly and Mo of Buchanan, Buchanan and Foster again without the right answers. And I am not disappointing Karen. Her parents have put her through the wringer on this wedding thing. It's going to go off without a hitch."

"Then a foreign divorce is your only chance. Even if we draw up new papers for your wife—"

His heart did a backflip at the unfamiliar association.

"—to sign there's no way we can get a judge to finalize the divorce before the next scheduled wedding."

"Fine. We'll do a quickie divorce *and* an Illinois divorce. I didn't get where I am by not covering all the bases."

Gil made his way through the boarding lines, the screening, the paper stamping. It was an absolute miracle he'd slid his passport into his carryon before leaving Chicago. At least one thing in the last week had gone right. Next on his list of calls was Karen. He had a little explaining to do, and then his office would have to cancel any upcoming appointments for at least the next few days. He'd have to work as best as he could from the ship. Not the most convenient arrangement so close to his wedding, but if he was willing to admit it to himself, seeing Pam again might just be worth aggravating his ulcers.

"Okay take a deep breath and start again." Michelle Bradford McEntire pushed Pam into the club chair and handed her a bottled water. She'd have rather given her friend something stronger but the nearest bar wasn't open yet and she didn't want to run out on deck in search of an open bar.

"I'm married."

"That's what you said before."

"She's been mumbling like a punch drunk parrot ever since she hung up from that call." Angie waved her arms in a show of despair. "She turned and walked away, muttering, *Houston we have a problem.* I had to run to keep up with her. Finally steered her toward the lounge and called you."

"I'm right here. No need to talk like I've just had a lobotomy," Pam finally uttered a little more clearly.

"Good, then tell us what's the story."

"I don't think good is the word I'm looking for." Pam sucked in a lungful of air and blew out a controlled breath. "My first husband is meeting me here after dinner."

Michelle wasn't sure who looked more stunned at this point, Pam, Angie, or herself. Of all the crazy scenarios she could have dreamed up, this wasn't anywhere on the horizon of her imagination. "Your first husband is going to be on this ship?"

Pam nodded.

"One helluva coincidence." Angie shrugged.

"Not a coincidence." A little more color in her complexion, Pam faced her friends. "He's getting married in a couple of weeks."

"Okay." Angie leaned back and crossed her arms. "You gotta admit at least *that's* a coincidence."

Pam ignored her. "He needed a copy of our divorce papers for his fiancée's lawyers and the prenup."

"Ooh, he's marrying money." Angie leaned forward again.

Pam continued to ignore her. "It looks like there was a miscommunication and neither of our divorce attorneys actually filed the papers."

Now Michelle understood the crazy muttering. "Which means you two are still legally married."

Pam's head bobbed up and down and slowly came to a halt. "Holy mackerel." She sprang up. "I need to get my hair done. Maybe a manicure." She glanced down at her sandaled feet. "And a pedicure. I can't wait for my appointment later in the week. I've been wearing this dress since the crack of dawn. I must look a mess."

"The dress is fine and your nails look great," Angie snapped, shaking her head.

"But not my hair?" Frowning at Angie, Pam's hands flew up to pat her casually pinned hair.

"Time out." Michelle raised her hands to her friends and stared at Pam. "Are you nuts? You look fine."

"Fine for what? I haven't seen this man since I was eighteen years old. There's a lot of gravity that has set in since then. I may not want him back, but I sure as hell want him to miss what he lost."

"Okay," Angie laughed. "That's the Pam we all know and love."

Michelle chuckled too, "Okay. Maybe you have a teeny tiny point. Wonder how soon the spa opens."

"Everything opens after we leave port."

Pam looked at her watch. She could hear the calypso band on deck playing. "I've got three hours till dinner."

A broad grin took over her face. Any sign of nerves or shock vanished and the tough, strong woman Michelle had come to depend on during one of the hardest episodes in her life was back.

"By the time I'm done at the salon," Pam dropped her hands to her waist, "Gilbert Daniel Harris won't know what hit him."

Gil had no idea where he was scheduled to dine tonight. Nor did he care. The only thing he could think of for the last few hours since stepping aboard this floating hotel was that he would be coming face to face with the first love of his life. Having dinner with a table of strangers held about as much appeal as dancing naked in a cactus patch. He'd opted for a quick bite at the top deck buffet.

The hastily made plans were to meet in the Lido

Lounge at 10pm. Rather than roam about searching out faces, he chose to have a seat at an empty table with an excellent view of the passersby to wait. With more than an hour before Pam made her appearance he switched from bourbon to cola. The first drink had steadied his nerves, any more would be overkill. For the next forty-five minutes he sipped his drink, munched on peanuts—more for something to do than because he was still hungry as he'd lost his appetite days ago—and watched assorted couples come and go. To distract himself he played a guessing game of who the passengers were and why were they travelling. Second honeymoon and retirement party seemed to be the top contenders. He wondered how many were seeking shipboard romances and if any—like him and Pam—would be needing shipboard divorces.

When the piano player arrived and made himself at home behind the keyboard, Gil was relieved for a chance to have something else to turn his attention to. After three or four songs he realized the distraction was more of a walk down memory lane than he was prepared for. Familiar love songs. Too many from the days when he and Pam were a crazy high school couple wrapped up in an intense case of puppy love. Of course at eighteen everything was intense. And dramatic. Every test, every date, every game. To the sheltered world of a high school senior in rural Georgia, every choice was to avoid being stuck forever in that godforsaken corner of the world. Baseball would be his ticket out. And it was. He'd been a nerdy kid trying desperately to study his way out of Georgia. In a stupid attempt for popular Pammy Watson to notice him, he tried out for the baseball team. At the time it had seamed much safer and less painful than football. No one was more surprised than him when it turned out he could not only play, he played incredibly well, and pitched even better. To the tune of a full ride scholarship to a division one college in a major city not within driving distance of the Georgia state line. He'd had it all. Star ball player and most popular kid in school went hand in hand. So did dating the head cheerleader, and he and Pam being voted prom King and

Queen. They were the golden couple. And so blasted in love. At least he thought they were. With the pressure to perform well for a career-making scholarship off his back, by summer they were hot and heavy and pretty near inseparable.

"Would you like another drink?" A pretty woman in dark slacks and a white shirt asked. The lounge was filling up and the wait staff was roaming about in full force.

"Another cola please."

She smiled, nodded and walked away. Young, pretty and according to her name tag, a name he couldn't pronounce from a country as behind the times as his own hometown. For a minute he paused to wonder what were this gal's dreams. When the waitress set the fresh drink in front of him, he signed off and added an obscene tip. Handing the bill back to her, he caught a flash of color moving closer from the bar.

"Pam." He actually pushed to his feet to watch her sway across the room. She still knew how to strut her stuff. Some things obviously never changed. Not her flamboyant style, her blinding smile, the I've-got-a-secret gleam in her eyes, or the fire in his stomach. Oh heavens, this was going to be way harder than he'd thought.

# CHAPTER FOUR

The least Gil Harris could have done was sprout a potbelly and lost his hair. Standing across the room, the grown up prom king could easily be running for president of the country. For all she knew, maybe he was. Tall and lean, with strong shoulders held straight. Not a stray pound in sight. Every strand of wavy hair might have been cut respectably short, but each one was still suitable for a woman's fingers to run through. Blast.

There was no missing the moment his gaze caught sight of her. That lazy grin that always made her stomach do calisthenics, teased at the corners of his mouth seconds before he stood and his lips curved into a full wattage smile. If he wasn't running for president, he should be. Hell, half the women in America would probably vote for him just to have someone decent to look at while they're favorite TV shows were being interrupted to lie about the state of the union.

Hoping her knees wouldn't give out on her, Pam pushed forward and did her best to flash a confident smile that hid just how nervous seeing her first ex-husband face to face made her. Not only had Gil grown up handsome, he'd grown up well mannered too. He'd always been nice, but she didn't remember him ever pulling out a chair for her. Of course that could have a lot to do with their only sitting in booths at Nell's diner.

"It's nice to see you," Gill waited for her to sit and then eased the chair closer to the low round table between them.

"Yes, it is." Okay. Now what did she say?

"Would you like something to drink?" He raised his arm and gestured for the waitress to come their way.

Torn between wanting a scotch on the rocks, double, or a diet cola, Pam figured she'd either have steady nerves or a clear head, but less chance than a snowball in hell of both.

"A Tom Collins?" He looked to her, the waitress standing beside him.

Tom Collins. Holy sleeping dogs. She hadn't tasted that cocktail since she'd left Georgia. One night a thousand years ago, they'd been curled up on the sofa at Gil's house making out more than watching TV, while some old black and white movie played in the background. Somewhere along the way while they pretended to pay attention to the film, a very elegant heroine in a sleek dress with a cigarette at the end of a prissy holder ordered a Tom Collins. In the back of his souped-up Chevy they drank the same local hooch everyone else did, but after that night, the few times they'd gone out with fake IDs and pretended to be grown up, she'd ordered a Tom Collins. The memories were still swirling dizzily in her mind when she realized Gil and the waitress were waiting for her. "Yes, thank you." Her stomach did another one of those flips and she worried if a clear head wouldn't have been a better choice.

"The lady will have a Tom Collins. I'll have a light beer. Whatever's on tap."

The young woman nodded her head and moved on to the next table. The lounge was beginning to fill with after dinner guests drawn to the music. The music. And why had she suddenly noticed that? The piano player was doing his best to channel Frank Sinatra or one of the other old time crooners. Right now he sounded a heck of a lot like Michael Bolton singing "How am I Supposed to Live Without You." Stiffening in her seat, she shoved all the high school memories sneaking out to play, back to the recesses of her mind where they belonged.

"I've updated my attorneys on our situation," Gil said. "We're hopeful this is all a misunderstanding, but realistically, we're going to need to do this from scratch again. We need to determine how much time we have to fix this…situation."

"I'm getting married in ten days when we dock in St.

Marteen. Can your lawyers sort this all out by then?" Fingers and toes crossed, she certainly hoped so.

"Depends on the ports of call." Gil pulled out his phone. "Give me a second to text my lawyer."

The guy has his lawyer's cell phone number on speed dial? Who the hell had Gilbert Harris become?

"That leaves us," he pulled a sheet of paper from his pocket and consulted it, "six ports before St. Maarten. I'm sending my lawyer a text with this data so he can determine if any of them do quickie divorces."

"That pretty much matches our married life."

The waitress returned and set the drinks on the table then walked away with Gil's room card and empty glass.

Waiting till the woman was safely out of hearing distance, Gil turned to face Pam. "Somehow I never actually looked at it that way."

"Well, if it takes nine days for a divorce and our marriage only lasted weeks..."

A soft rumble of Gil's too familiar laughter caught her ear and sent her insides fluttering yet again. Blast, why did he still have to sound so good.

"You may want to reconsider that *weeks* thing," he smiled.

The chuckle that erupted from her own lips took her by surprise. He was of course right. Technically they'd been married all these years. And through all her husbands. If she didn't laugh with him she'd probably cry. "This is one heck of a mess. Does your fiancée know?"

Gil's head bobbed up and down.

"How's she taking it?"

"She's a sensible woman."

"That didn't answer my question." Pam took her first sip of the nostalgic drink, appreciating the calming tendrils of the smooth swallow.

"These things happen." Gil shrugged. "She knows it was neither of our faults. But she is a bit concerned about the wedding plans falling apart if we don't resolve this quickly."

"Big wedding?"

He nodded again. "She's an only child."

And if there's a prenup, odds were Angie was right and the fiancée came with money too. A pedigree wouldn't be a surprise either. Gil looked like someone who had learned to fit in well on the right side of the tracks. Something his mother had made very clear—often—that would not happen if he'd stayed married to her. And blast if it didn't still sting that the woman had been right.

"What about your fiancé? Have you had a chance to tell him?"

"Not exactly." Pam's mouth went dry and the contents of her stomach soured. Dinner had lasted over an hour and a half, and not once had she come up with the words to mention she was still married. To her first husband. It had been a group effort to free her up for this little visit. Kirk had gotten Leo and his brother all excited about checking out the casino. Leo's sister-in-law, a professor of English Literature and a bit on the stiff side, had been unwittingly just as helpful coming down with a headache and retiring to her room. The remaining three women, Pam, Michelle, and Angie, were supposed to be at the late cabaret show. Pam, of course, was not. "I'm hoping we can get all of this settled and never have to say a word."

It was pretty clear by the way Gil's brows rose slightly on his forehead that he didn't see eye to eye with her philosophy. "Considering the impending deadline, that plan could be a little risky."

Peering over the rim of her glass as he took a long swallow of beer, Pam dared to look him in the eye. For the first time all evening, she was filled with a surprising sense of calm. The ambitious boy she'd once known, now had the look of eagles in his eyes. If anyone could resolve this mess in less than ten days, Gil and his speed dial lawyers would be the ones to pull it off.

"Pam."

At the sound of the familiar voice calling her name in the not very far distance, her heart skipped a beat before battering full speed ahead into her ribs. Out of the thousands of people on this massive ship, there had to be at least a dozen women named Pam, but only one whose voice she would recognize.

"Honey," Leo's voice sounded a little stronger, closer.

Pam didn't dare glance behind her, she knew that voice too well. Sucking in a breath, she leaned to one side and without looking Gil in the face, managed to spit out the words, "As much as I hate to say this, I think my past and my future are about to collide."

Gil wasn't sure how to respond, but he was willing to bet this year's bonus that the man making his way toward them and calling Pam's name was the future Gil was about to collide with.

"Please don't say anything," Pam whispered seconds before pushing to her feet and turning to face the man now frantically waving in her direction.

"I thought you were at the show with the girls?" The man, clearly more than a few years older than Pam, barely cast a glance in Gil's direction.

"I thought you were in the casino?" she dodged.

"Kirk's cleaning up at the roulette wheel, but the black jack table wasn't as kind to me so I decided to take a little walk and change my luck. Where are Michelle and Angie?" The guy pretended to be looking around for the first time, but as sure as Gil knew Georgia grew peaches, he knew that Pam's future had already seen him and probably calculated everything about him down to his height, weight, and net worth.

Pam slid one hand onto her hip and waved the other arm in what Gil assumed was the general direction of the ship's theater. He wondered if the fiancé knew that when Pam perched her left hand on her hip, tilted her head slightly, and smiled rather than talked, she had something to hide. Or at least she used to. And since he knew she was trying to hide him, he'd guess one more thing hadn't changed.

Mr. Fiancé chose to no longer ignore Gil's presence and

stuck out his hand. "Leo Dixon, nice to meet you."

"Gil Harris. Likewise."

"Oh, where are my manners?" Pam pivoted on one foot, linked her left arm with her fiancé's and kept right on grinning. "Honey, Gil and I went to school together."

"Really? And where was that?"

Without skipping a beat, both Pam and Gil chorused, "Podunk County High," then burst into laughter.

"Sorry," Pam shook her head, swallowing her mirth. "There wasn't a kid in the county who didn't want to get out of town and live somewhere else—"

"Anywhere else," Gil added without thinking.

Pam nodded. "Anywhere else. I think that nickname must have been with the school since before any of us were born."

The tension in Leo's shoulders eased slightly. The unrehearsed response had been too sincere not be the truth. "Quite a coincidence bumping into each other, here of all places."

"You have no idea," Pam muttered before leaning closer into her companion's side. "We should go find Kirk."

"He's a big boy, I'm sure he can find us if he wants to." Before Pam could do anything about it, Leo had descended into the empty chair beside them. "So, Gil, are you here with the wife?"

"I'm here by myself." Leo's brows creased momentarily and Pam's eyes widened, so Gil hurried on. "I have some business to take care of on this trip, but with my wedding only a few weeks away, my fiancée couldn't join me."

At those last words, Leo's shoulders finally relaxed all the way. "Well, that is a shame. Did she go to high school with you two as well?"

"No," Gil shook his head. Karen was as far from a southern country girl as a human being could get. "She's from Chicago."

"Is that where you live now?" Pam asked, releasing her hold on Leo.

"Yeah."

"I recently did some consulting work in Chicago." Leo leaned back and crossed his ankle over his knee. "Didn't expect to like the city as much as I did."

"It gets rough in winter, but the rest of the year makes up for it."

"What do you do?"

"Securities and Investment broker."

"Really?" Leo's eyes widened slightly. "Familiar with Investco Brokerage?"

"Yes." The world couldn't be that small. "I work there."

"Hmm." This time Leo's chin bobbed and his gaze settled heavily on Gil. "Allister Smythe and I go back a long way."

"There you are." A tall guy with a tan that said he didn't live anywhere near a cold city like Chicago, came up beside them. If this man was friends with Pam and privy to the awkward situation, his casual expression gave nothing away.

"Pull up a chair," Leo offered gesturing to an empty seat behind him. "Kirk McEntire, this is Gil Harris, an old friend of Pam's. From high school. Turns out an associate of an old friend of mine as well."

Kirk turned to face Gil. "Small world."

*And getting smaller by the minute.*

"Nice to meet you." Kirk extended his hand, a firm but not too powerful grip said a lot about why the man's expression gave nothing away. Pulling a nearby chair over, he sat and turned to Pam. "Michelle just texted me. The show is over and they want to know where to meet up. That's when I noticed I'd lost Leo."

"I found him," Pam deadpanned. "Maybe we should see what's happening on deck. I understand these ships are overflowing with late night buffets of fabulous foods."

"Nonsense," Leo chimed in. "Have the girls meet us here. I'm looking to find out more about where my pretty Pam came from."

"Oh, that won't—" Pam started.

"I should get back to—" Gil tried to help.

Kirk's phone buzzed. "It's Michelle."

"Lido lounge. Tell them we're saving seats." Leo didn't wait for an answer, he stood, walked over to a table with an extra chair.

Pinching her eyes shut, Pam's face blanched ever so slightly and Gil had an uneasy feeling that the next few days were going to be one heck of a ride.

# CHAPTER FIVE

**"H**e's not bad looking."

Pam kicked her sandals off and flopped onto the single bed. "No."

At the small vanity area, Angie slipped off her earrings then ran a brush through her hair. "I have to admit, I'd let that man eat crackers in my bed."

And so would Pam. It had taken her a lot of years to get Gil out of her mind. From the day he'd asked her out for burgers the first week of senior year, everything else in her life seemed to just be better. By the time the homecoming dance had come around they were officially a couple and she was the envy of half the girls in the school. By Valentine's Day they were inseparable and she was so darn happy that she didn't even care about the rumors flying about. A few uglier than others, and almost all having something to do with bleachers, the locker room, or the backseat of his Chevy.

In late spring, just before prom, Jimmy Joe Lawson had the bad luck to repeat one of those rumors within earshot of Gil. Not a single person in or out of school dared whisper a contrary word after he'd slammed Jimmy Joe against a locker and threatened to wash out his mouth with toilet water until the jock learned how to speak about Gil's girlfriend. She didn't need to wait for Gil to be crowned prom king to know he was the guy for her. He'd been her knight in shining armor and she'd loved him with everything she had.

"So why did you kick him out of bed?"

"It wasn't like that."

"So tell me." Angie sat, legs folded, on the bed. "How

was it?"

"We were young. Very young. I'd turned eighteen in June. In July we ran off to Vegas to get married. Drove cross country." She couldn't help the smile that tugged at her mouth. Running away to marry her prince had been like a fairytale come true.

"I'm guessing by that grin on your face, the honeymoon was pretty memorable."

Three more marriages and she'd never been able to recreate that fairytale high. She'd decided long ago that the euphoria was more because of age than love. After only a few hours with Gil in a crowded lounge, she wasn't so sure anymore.

"Yoo hoo." Angie waved her hand in front of Pam's face. "Star spangled honeymoon?"

"Sorry. Yeah. But there wasn't much for a young man to do in our neck of the woods except work in one of the factories. Gil wanted more. I used to call him George for George Bailey from the It's a Wonderful Life movie. He wanted to see the world."

"And you didn't?" Angie's brows contorted with confusion.

Pam shrugged. That wasn't the point. "He had a baseball scholarship and a few grants lined up. When we got home from Vegas his mother pointed out the fine print." *Upon every good fairytale a wicked witch must fall.* "Being married disqualified him for enough of the money that he wouldn't have been able to go to college. He'd have been stuck in Porterville."

"So you two got a divorce instead?" Angie's brow creased with confusion again.

Pam couldn't tie him down to her and that miserable little town with no future. She had to let him go off to school without her in August, but it had only taken until Halloween for her to know she had to get away from Porterville. Gil had been better off without her, and if she'd stayed around till he came home at Thanksgiving she might never have gotten the courage to leave. "It made sense at the time. We knew we were young. Foolish. Puppy love."

"I don't know." Angie shook her head. "There's a lot to be said for high school sweethearts."

"We only dated our senior year."

"That's still high school last time I looked."

"Doesn't matter. He's done well for himself. I made the right choice." *Right choice.* If she repeated it more often maybe it wouldn't be so hard to spit out.

"So this divorce thing was your idea?" Angie's voice rose with incredulity. Not like she didn't believe her, more like Angie thought Pam had lost more than her marbles.

"Actually, it was his mother's suggestion. But she was right. Most couples wait until they finish school to get married. Hell, today they wait even longer than that."

"So she wanted the two of you to remarry after he graduated?"

She and Gil had thought so at first. Even bought into the idea with Pam working and saving it would all work out, but after he'd gone she'd learned his mother's true agenda. Mrs. Harris wanted someone better for her baby boy. Once Pam realized the woman was right, she couldn't spend four more years listening to his mother carry on about how wonderful his life was in college. All the parties, the fun, the opportunities for a single man. The bright future Pam would only hold him back from. Oh, how those words had pricked at her back then.

"I wouldn't go that far." This time Pam almost laughed. The hurt had faded years ago. "At first that was what she'd said—until Gil was gone. She'd made it pretty clear she was hoping he'd meet some nice smart college girl and forget about me. She thought he could do better than the head cheerleader waiting tables for a living."

"Well, for what it's worth I think any man is better than lucky to have you, but that doesn't explain what kept you apart."

More than once Pam had asked herself the same question. What if she had stayed in Porterville and waited out the four years? If she'd put up with the stupid town gossip. Like Mrs. Harris had chirped to anyone who would listen, would they only have wound up divorced just the same?

Gil toed off his shoes and dropped down on the king size bed. The small group of Pam's friends had grown to include two brothers, a couple from Peoria celebrating their silver wedding anniversary, and Leo's niece and nephew. One drink had led to two and shortly after midnight the entire gang had moved to the disco. Tapping his foot to the energetic tunes, he'd been tempted more than once to grab Pam and spin her around on the dance floor. Pam had needed a couple of credits for graduation to make up for having failed biology back in her sophomore year. The safest bet seemed to be the swing dance class that counted as physical education. To this day he didn't know how she'd roped him into taking it with her as one of his senior year electives. The baseball team had ribbed him mercilessly over it. But it turned out they both had rhythm—and fun.

To tamp down the music in his feet, he spent a good chunk of the evening chatting with Leo's nephew, Brent. With a girl back home, the kid seemed more concerned about keeping an eye on his younger sister. Not that she needed it. Only eighteen, she struck him as being incredibly sensible and perfectly content to hang out with her parents and the rest of the old farts. A world away from where he and Pam had been fresh out of high school. Though Brent in many ways reminded Gil of himself at that age. A charming young man, a senior at Stanford, the kid had a future as bright as the North Star. Gil remembered those days well. He'd done an internship at Karen's fathers' company the summer before senior year. Immediately following that, he'd been offered a full time position. By graduation his career path was laid out for him. No where to go but up. The high hopes of a starry eyed kid. At least those dreams were rooted more heavily in reality than the pie in the sky expectations of two teens thinking they were old enough to play house.

His phone dinged with a text. What he'd hoped were

answers from his lawyer turned out to be a missed message from Karen. DAD IS BREATHING FIRE. NOTHING NEW. HOW ARE YOU?

TIRED. NOTHING NEW HERE YET. He supposed he should say something appropriate, like miss you, but somehow tonight the small talk didn't come.

WISH YOU WERE HERE TO DEAL WITH DAD AND I WAS THERE SOAKING UP THE SUN ☺

Chuckling, he just bet she did. Karen's relationship with her overbearing father had been underwhelming most of her life. Now that she was *finally* getting married, instead of easing back, Allister Smythe was even more of a typhoon force, demanding every small detail for the elaborate wedding meet with his approval. A few times Gil had been tempted to tell his future father-in-law to take a long walk on a short pier and whisk Karen away for a small wedding with only a few friends. Always the people pleaser, Karen had insisted that he didn't want to know what it was like to have Allister Smythe on your bad side. ME TOO.

LIAR LIAR PANTS ON FIRE. She answered.

Gil smiled at the phone. He'd been with Investco Brokerage a few years before he'd advanced enough to be included in Smythe family events. The antithesis of her domineering and demanding father, Karen's breezy smile and easygoing nature had been a magnet for a man who worked more hours than he slept, for more years than he could count. He was a lucky man to be marrying his best friend. Again. SLEEP WELL.

YOU TOO. NIGHT.

DON'T LET THE BED BUGS BITE. He'd said that one night, stupefied with exhaustion, and Karen had laughed so hard that it had become almost a ritual when he was on a business trip. Though this was a different sort of business, there was comfort in the familiar.

Too tired to change, he set his phone on the nightstand and leaned back on the covers. Tomorrow would be a full day at sea before reaching Nassau. He didn't want to think about what the day would be like. Leo had insisted that Gil join them for breakfast tomorrow and despite his best efforts to beg off explaining he needed to work, somehow he'd left the group agreeing to meet them in front of the main deck dining room at nine. Leo seemed to be a pretty nice guy. The sort of fellow who would probably make Pam happy. Stable, confident, sociable. There was just one irritating little issue. Every time he laid a hand on Pam, Gil had to swallow the urge to shout, "Keep your hands off my wife." Blast, if fate didn't have one heck of a sense of humor.

# CHAPTER SIX

S ince the crack of dawn, Pam had been wide awake and calculating excuses in her head to get out of having breakfast with her… husband and her fiancé. "Do you think they'd believe I fell overboard?"

Elbow over her eyes, Angie mumbled, "Not without sirens blaring and someone screaming Oscar Oscar Oscar."

"Who the blazes is Oscar?"

"Michelle once told me that was the code for man overboard on this cruise line."

"And you remembered?" Pam wondered sometimes what sort of crazy data processing went on in her friend's busy head.

Angie shrugged. "It's a gift."

"Maybe I could come down with the Asian flu."

"We're in the Caribbean."

"That time of the month?"

Angie peeled her arm away from her face and turned to look at Pam with one eye. "Do you seriously want me to announce to the world that you're spending the day in our room because you have cramps?"

Pam yanked the pillow out from under her head and hugged it against her. "I suppose not."

"Good choice." Angie's arm resumed its place over her eyes. "There are lots of couples who make better friends after the divorce than during the marriage. Why don't you just stop thinking of him as your ex husband and think of him as a new friend? Maybe that will make the rest of this trip easier."

Slinging her legs over the side of the bed and sitting up, Pam had to admit Angie might have a point. Gil Harris was just a man, and she knew how to handle men. Leo Dixon was her future. All she had to do was find a friendly island for a divorce and get on with her life. "You're absolutely right. What we had is water under the bridge. It's after seven. I'm going to grab a shower and get dressed. Maybe take a walk on deck before breakfast."

"Sounds good." Angie rolled over and mumbled to the wall. "Wake me when you're done."

Pam managed to shower and dress in record time, especially for her. Of course it helped that she'd opted to skip doing her hair or putting on her face till after coffee. Curled up under the blankets, Angie looked so peaceful that Pam didn't have the heart to wake her. The appointed meeting time was more than an hour away. Instead of waking her friend, Pam opted to run up to the coffee shop. She had a feeling the early morning would be more palatable for Angie with a warm dose of caffeine, and maybe a Danish. Pam laughed to herself—or a Dane, tall, blonde, with blue eyes and a killer smile, but she wasn't too likely to find one of those for her friend on this side of the Atlantic.

Checking her pocket for the room card, Pam stepped into the hall and eased the door shut.

"Good Morning." Mary Jane and Eddie, the couple from Peoria celebrating their anniversary, stood beside her. "Heading for breakfast?"

"Uh, no. Thought I'd get my roommate some coffee to help her wake up."

"Breakfast in bed is always a fun way to start the day. I'm sure she'll appreciate it." Holding hands with her husband of twenty-five years, Mary Jane flashed a smile and stepped around Pam in the direction of the rear elevators and the dining rooms. "See you later I'm sure."

The coffee shop was in the front end of the ship. Pam had made it about twenty feet when a door ahead opened and out stepped brothers Taylor and Brian. "Good morning."

Served her right for not at least putting on some blush and lipstick. "Morning."

"Going to breakfast?"

"No. Just getting coffee for my roommate."

Taylor turned to his brother. "Next time remind me to leave you home and bring a thoughtful roommate instead."

"I could say the same about you," the brother shot back.

Pam shook her head, siblings. "Gotta run."

"See ya later," the two brothers followed in the same direction as the anniversary couple.

"I'm sure," she called over her shoulder, then mumbled, "You and everyone else on this boat."

"Hi." A seriously perky voice fell in step beside her. Emily, Leo's niece.

Lord love a duck, was the entire ship berthing on the deck five? "Morning."

"Heading to the coffee shop?"

Poised to say no, Pam stuttered a second at the realization they would both be heading in the same direction. Of all her choices, she was glad Emily was the one settling for coffee. "Actually, yes."

"Me too. I'm not much of a breakfast person, even if it is the most important meal of the day."

"Also good for your metabolism. Not that you need any help now, but another twenty years and you'll be in constant battle with it."

"My mother grumbles all the time about her weight and how when she was young..." Emily's voice trailed off and she looked about ready to do that teenage eye roll thing but instead let out a resolved sigh.

"Where's your brother?" Pam turned the corner by the elevator bays.

"Sound asleep. He stayed out after the party broke up. I wouldn't hold breakfast up waiting for him."

The elevator doors opened and a throng of early morning risers stepped out, and they walked in. Pam studied the elevator floor and the day of the week name plate on the carpet. "Do you think that's automatic or manual?"

Emily glanced down. "I'm betting manual."

"Hmm." Pam wondered. Everything was automated these days. She found it hard to believe that a human being had the job of elevator day changer. Then again, life on a cruise ship wasn't exactly the same as the starship Enterprise. "You're a freshman in college, right?"

"Technically I'm a sophomore. I had enough AP courses to skip a semester and a half."

Smart. "Do you have a major?"

The kid's face lit up. "Mechanical Engineering."

The elevator came to a sharp stop along with Pam's attitude. Emily was a wisp of a thing. Probably about five foot and two or three inches tall in her stocking feet. Average figure. Pretty face. Not what Pam envisioned with the word Mechanical Engineer attached. She couldn't help but wonder how different things might have been if she'd believed herself smart enough to go to college. "Good for you."

"What do you do?"

"Admin for the editor of a newspaper. Used to work with Michelle before she moved to California." She'd hated to see Michelle go, but when all the dust finally settled after Kirk finished turning the paper around, Pam had been one of only a handful of employees to still have jobs.

"They seem like a nice couple."

They reached the coffee shop. "Michelle and Kirk? Oh yeah. He was the hatchet man sent to trim the fat from the paper I work for."

"Uh oh."

Laughing Pam reached for a Styrofoam cup. "Oh yeah. It was nuts. Turns out they'd actually met before on a cruise."

Emily filled her cup with a tea bag and hot water. "Talk about a small world."

Still chuckling, Pam shook her head. From where she stood the world was getting a whole heck of a lot smaller and smaller every day.

Up since the first blink of sunrise, Gil checked his phone for the umpteenth time. There wasn't a hen's chance in a fox den that he'd get a decent night sleep until he had a concrete game plan in place. Not something based on hypothetical possibilities or probabilities.

Not for the first time since being sucked into the whirlpool of activity by Pam's fiancé and friends, had Gil debated how bad would it look if he simply didn't show up for breakfast. Wasn't the entire idea of a cruise vacation to leave schedules and rules behind and let loose and have fun? Not that he had any intention of letting loose or having fun. The plan was to nail down the details of what happened—or didn't happen, determine their accurate marital status, and if necessary, procure a legal divorce, then get hightail it back to Chicago where he belonged.

"Hey man, how goes it?" It took Gil a few seconds to realize the voice was talking to him. Kirk was coming off the bottom step of the midship grand circular staircase.

"Good morning." Gil hadn't pictured Kirk as the sort to sleep in, but damp hair and the light scent of shipboard soap said otherwise. "Ready for breakfast?"

"Starving. Did a short workout and jog around the track. I could eat an elephant's rump."

"I see." Gil smiled and fell in step beside Kirk. This was someone more like who he would have pictured Pam marrying. Although, now that he thought about it, Leo probably would have been much like himself or Kirk fifteen years or so ago.

"Do you play handball?" Kirk asked.

"Used to."

"They have a great court here if you want to give it a go."

Working off a little nervous energy might not be a bad idea, even if he hadn't set foot in a handball court in at least a decade. "You're on."

"Great. We'll see what the women have planned and whatever sounds the most boring is when I'll schedule the court."

Tossing and turning last night, Gil had been so focused on facing everyone again this morning that it hadn't even occurred to him to consider the plans for the rest of the day. Except for the handball game, lying low—and alone—held the most appeal. Not to mention he did need to get some work done. What little he could do on his cell phone and the iPad that he always carried might be limited, but he couldn't ignore his work all together. Not if he was about to spend a month on a South Pacific honeymoon. Of course he'd told all of that to Leo last night and it had gotten him nowhere. Who the heck was this guy? Gil was going to have to sign up for the internet package he saw in the daily newsletter left on his bed. The price teetered precariously between extortion and usury, but he hadn't gotten where he was today by waiting for other people to do his legwork. It was time for Mr. Google and him to spend a little time together.

A few feet ahead, Michelle stood alone at the entry to the main deck dining room. The only dining floor serving a full breakfast. She was an attractive woman, tall, slender, brown hair, brown eyes, but the second she spotted her husband, those average brown eyes lit with delight. The broad smile that worked its way across her face transformed her from merely attractive to absolutely stunning. Impulse had him turning to his new handball partner.

The perfect bookend, Kirk bestowed a blinding smile on his wife. The sheer adoration in his eyes hit Gil like a high voltage shock. Had he ever once looked at Karen that way? The two came together like a Hallmark commercial. The kiss was brief, chaste, but the searing heat in their locked gazes had Gil thirsting for an icy beverage, maybe even a cold shower.

"Except for Leo's niece and nephew, the others are already at the table." Michelle eased away from Kirk, but held onto his hand.

What was it about married people and hand holding on cruises? Most of the married people Gil knew rarely spent any time in the same room, never mind holding hands and grinning like newlyweds. *Like newlyweds.* Soon he and Karen would be newlyweds. Obviously he knew they were getting married. He'd spent the better part of the last year nodding his head at all the ridiculous details his future mother-in-law set before him and Karen. From the ribbon color for the church pews to the complimentary tablecloth hue for each dessert table. Until last year he didn't know there was such a thing as a dessert table. Yet somehow only now did he realize getting married led to being newlyweds.

Following Kirk and Michelle to the table, the word newlywed continued to bounce around in his head. No matter how hard he tried, there was no conjuring up images of him and Karen behaving like a besotted newly married couple. The only picture of post marital bliss that continued to creep into his thoughts was that of another bride and another groom. A very, very long time ago. *Blast.*

# CHAPTER SEVEN

There was no need to look up, no need to pull her attention away from her fiancé. As sure as she knew she was a natural redhead, Pam knew Gil had entered the dining room. She'd hoped Michelle and Kirk would arrive first so she could avoid her ex taking the seat beside her. Not that there was any reason to think he'd want to sit beside her. And of course, after her early morning resolution to only think of Gil as a new friend, where he sat shouldn't—didn't—matter. Still she'd hoped hope maybe fate would cut her a little slack this morning.

"Sorry we're running a bit late." Kirk escorted his wife around the table and pulled the seat out beside Pam.

She bit back a sigh of relief and told herself she needed to do something nice for Kirk. Maybe gift his wife with some pretty lingerie. Not that it mattered. From what she'd seen last night, it was a miracle the heat in their gazes hadn't set the ship on fire.

"Good morning, everyone." Gil took the only remaining empty seat between Angie and Kirk.

At her ex's appearance, Pam found herself reaching over and grabbing hold of Leo's free hand. Whether she' done it for support or reassurance, she wasn't sure. "Did you sleep well?"

Angie's eyes widened and Pam squeezed hers shut. Any other person, anywhere in the world, under any other circumstance and that would have been a perfectly normal question. But asking her not so ex husband whose mere presence on the ship had lost her hours of precious beauty sleep, was probably on the top ten things not to ask a person you'd once savored waking up beside.

"Well enough, thank you." His response came out stiff and formal, and Pam wondered if his night had been that rough or was he merely playing a part.

"That sounds rather ominous." Leo glanced up, setting the brief breakfast menu down.

"Not really. I have a great deal of business on my mind." He cast a brief look in Pam's direction. "Hoping to get set up today with internet and start getting down to work."

"Surely, you're not going to work the entire cruise?" Leo's sister-in-law Nancy looked at him aghast. With her husband also a tenured professor, Nancy and George had a history of traveling during school breaks. From what Pam understood, Nancy was more the art gallery and museum type who relished far away places and ancient cultures. She'd only fussed briefly at the idea of floating on a boat for two weeks with little entertainment for the mind. Apparently to her brokerage business didn't qualify as brain food.

Gil reached for the nearby menu. "I'm afraid I probably am."

"I suppose it's better than being bored." Stone-faced, the skeletal woman shrugged a shoulder.

"Now, Nancy. There will be plenty of interesting things to do and see." George patted his wife's hand. "This trip is supposed to be fun."

On the word fun, Pam's gaze reflexively shifted to Gil in time to collide with his. Just a new friend, she repeated silently to herself and smiled. "George, what do you and Nancy have on the agenda for today?"

"There's trivia in an hour. That could be interesting," the dour woman answered and Pam did her best to keep smiling. A luxury ocean liner in the sunny Caribbean and Nancy wanted to stay indoors and play trivia.

"I noticed some of the crew setting up these electronic gadgets for bingo. Looked interesting, and they mentioned some decent cash prizes," George added. "We could do that this afternoon."

"As long as we're free for the afternoon trivia," his wife answered.

"They do trivia twice a day?" Angie asked, looking less than impressed at the idea.

"Oh yes." Nancy's hands gestured with her first sign of enthusiasm. Her expression only slightly more relaxed. "And in the evening there's music trivia, though I suspect it will be pop music."

Once again, Pam's gaze shifted to Gil and this time she caught his shoulders shaking slightly as he buried his head and his laughter in the menu.

"They have a pretty nice game room. Maybe we men could get in a round of poker?" Leo had let go of Pam's hand and placed it on her knee. The gesture caught her by surprise. He didn't usually like any public display of affection. Even ones hidden under a table. She almost felt as though he were staking his claim. Polite society's version of peeing on her leg.

"I did notice a napkin folding class after trivia." Nancy's gaze passed from Angie, to Michelle, and settled on Pam. "That could prove useful. Perhaps we girls could do that while the guys get in a couple of hands of cards."

Michelle looked at her husband, her eyes pleading for help. Angie choked on the sip of water she'd just taken, and now Gil was staring straight at Pam, sucking in his lips to contain his humor. The mere sight of him trying so hard not to laugh out loud at the itinerary designed for blue-haired-old-ladies so enthusiastically laid out before her had Pam forgetting the boredom she was facing and instead struggling not to laugh herself.

"Do you play cards?" Leo asked Gil.

He shook his head. "Not much."

Pam almost dropped her fork. While on their honeymoon, Gil had tripled his meager bank roll playing cards in Vegas. Gil had an uncanny mind for remembering numbers. What cards had been played, who was holding what and which were still in the deck. If they hadn't been otherwise occupied most of the time, he could have walked away from any casino with a small fortune. When she dared look in his direction, he gave her a half-hearted shrug of a shoulder and then taking a second to make sure no one else was looking his way, he winked at her. The little sneak.

"Actually," piercing her husband with a dangerous gleam, Michelle leaned into him, "I noticed some interesting poolside activities today and thought we could do those."

"Yes." Kirk nodded his head, probably as eager as Pam was to get out of an afternoon of trivia or bingo. "Poolside sounds good."

It was all Pam could do not to bust out laughing. Apparently Nancy had everyone grasping at more entertaining straws. There were a few poolside events on today's list. Line dancing, which if that's what Michelle had in mind might actually be fun. Otherwise, poor Kirk was about to participate in the fun-filled Belly Flop Contest. Or was today Sexiest Man?

"I thought I'd make friends with a deck chair and catch up on my reading," Angie said with a slightly nervous smile.

Pam almost shook her head. There would be no loosening up on this ship if Angie kept her nose in a book.

"The ladies are right." Leo looked to George. "A little fresh air and sunshine would be good for all of us."

Lifting her chin Nancy wore a well-fitted air of intellectual superiority. "As long as I get to do my trivia, I suppose a little suntan could be a nice souvenir."

"Atta girl." Pam shot the woman an unappreciated thumbs up. "Let the fun begin."

Fifteen minutes on the internet had been enough for Gil to discover the only port for same day divorces on their itinerary was the Dominican Republic. In nine days. A dual signed divorce with a single representative would work if they didn't mind waiting twenty-one days for final decree. If the goal was a four-hour final divorce decree, both parties needed to go before the Caribbean judge. Which meant, barring some Hail Mary play by Gil's attorneys, he wasn't going to be getting off this floating hotel any time soon.

Next on his list, Leo Dixon. While scrolling through the running lists of men with the same name, eliminating the too young and too old, Gil's phone beeped with a text message.

HAVE SOME ANSWERS. CALL OR EMAIL?

About bloody time. Gil tapped his response. EMAIL AND ATTACH ALL DOCUMENTATION.

The answer seemed to take longer than a simple yes or okay required. Finally his screen lit up: ON ITS WAY

More seconds ticked by at the pace of a lame racehorse. Considering what the ship was charging, the internet speed seemed woefully slow. More in line with antiquated dial up then tolerable DSL. The concept of high speed seemed to completely elude the ship's technology.

His impatience was finally rewarded with an incoming mail. Anticipation and dread warred with each other, moving his finger to the enter key in equally slow motion. Attached was the original divorce agreement signed by him, the same document signed the following day by Pamela, and a profuse letter of apology from Pamela's then attorney. Quickly scanning the words for the high points, his stomach dipped low in his belly before bouncing back. He'd known deep down what Pam had said would be true. Known something had to have gone wrong. Known that inevitably the official conclusion would be that they were not divorced and he was going to have to stay on this ship with Pam and her fiancé for more than a week. Still, he'd stubbornly held on to the hope of finding a miraculous response.

Instead all he read was well scripted legal mumbo jumbo. AKA an apology. Bottom line, an inept legal assistant had misunderstood the instructions and rather than have Pam sign the copy Gil had already signed, she printed a clean copy for Pam to sign and returned it to Gil's lawyer. Gil's lawyer in turn followed up with the assistant who informed them the error would be corrected. Further research uncovered Gil's lawyer had called out the error on the same day the partners from Pam's firm had terminated the assistant. Aware she'd made several serious errors, the partners had thought they'd caught them all. Clearly they had not. Now Gil and Pam were most definitely, beyond any doubt, absolutely, and positively, still married.

The remainder of the body of the email from his lawyer basically informed him of what he already knew. The best option for a divorce in time for both Pam and Gil's weddings would be on the island of Hispaniola, home to both the Dominican Republic and Haiti. His attorneys were making all arrangements, including transportation from port to the Dominican capital city of Santo Domingo. The entire effort needed to be timed carefully. Nearly a two hour ride in each direction from the ship, four hours for final decree, and only nine hours in port. For all their sakes he hoped the four-hour promise was not of the 'manana' variety. He didn't know a Latin culture that kept to a schedule. One of Karen's dearest friends had worked for an American school somewhere in South America. One of the many oddities on her orientation list was if invited to dinner by a resident family, do not arrive on time or the teacher would most likely find the hostess still in her bathrobe. Lord he hoped the four hours was based on the American standard of telling time.

Another beep sounded on his phone. This time it was Kirk. HAVE THE COURTS IN 30. YOU STILL ON?

Was he? He hadn't even touched any of the business waiting for his attention. He also needed to find Pam and fill her in on the latest information. But either way, thirty minutes more or less wasn't going to change anything. At least, for a little while longer, he could leave Pam with the same small misguided hope he'd had, that they really had been divorced all these years.

I'M IN. MEET YOU THERE. If nothing else for the next hour or so he could beat the hell out of a little ball and keep his mind off what would go down next.

# CHAPTER EIGHT

This was the way to spend the day. Like most redheads, for Pam the sun wasn't usually her friend. But slathered in SPF 70 sunscreen, in a one-piece swimsuit, wearing a hat with a brim as wide as the deck, and a narrow swath of shade covering most of her, she couldn't think of any place more relaxing.

"I'll have another BBC please." Michelle held out her empty glass to the passing waiter who paused to ask the rest of the ladies if they needed refills.

"Diet cola," Angie said, holding out her empty glass as well.

Nancy followed suit. "BBC for me too."

Needing to keep her wits, Pam kept to her vow of giving up the hard stuff on this trip. "I'll have lemonade please."

All the empties perched on his tray, the waiter nodded, mumbled something about returning shortly, and spun away.

"I have to admit." Nancy leaned back with a smile on her face. "This is definitely better than bingo. Especially that Baileys milkshake."

"There's no milk in it," Angie softly corrected from her lounger beside Nancy.

"Whatever. It's delicious. So." Nancy shaded her eyes with her hand and looked to Michelle. "What else is on the horizon for today?"

A cheeky grin teased at one side of Michelle's lips. "Well…"

"I knew it." Pam blurted. Slapping her hands together and smiling, she sprang up straight in her seat. "Which is it?"

"That depends on how many beers I can get Kirk to drink before the first event."

"Oh this is going to be interesting." Pam leaned back. "So very."

Angie stared pointedly at her two friends while she casually spread sunscreen on her arms. "Anyone want to fill the rest of us in on your little secret?"

"Ladies," A deep voice announced.

Pam opened her eyes to see Kirk casting a shadow over his wife. Gil standing directly behind him.

"I convinced Gil here that it made more sense to rinse off in the pool than to head back to his room for a shower." Kirk flung a white towel from around his neck onto the deck beside his wife's chair and turned to Gil. "Last one in picks up the drink tab tonight."

Like a shot Kirk crossed the deck with Gil barely half a step behind him. The two men barked with laughter like a couple of teens playing hooky from school. She didn't know why, but seeing Gil so relaxed and having fun made her smile. All these years this was what she'd hoped had become of his world. The loss had been easier to swallow if she imagined him somewhere else, happy, enjoying life, love, maybe even raising little Gilberts. Ones who looked just like him, impish grin and all.

At the edge of the pool the two men hollered like Tarzan and leapt high in the air with their knees tucked to their chins. Landing dead center of the mostly empty space they sent flowing waves of water across the pool, over the side and onto half the sunbathers. Teens playing might have been too mature a description.

"Men," Nancy muttered. "Speaking of which. I guess mine are still in the game room playing cards."

"Or waiting for you at trivia," Michelle added.

A wry grin came over Nancy's lips. "Oops. Guess I missed that one."

At that less than contrite announcement, the waiter appeared with more drinks and Nancy's smile grew even wider. Less than twenty-four hours into the trip and already Pam had created a monster. Or an alcoholic. Only time would tell.

Michelle waved the waiter over. "Bring my husband a Bud Light." She turned to Pam. "Any idea what Gil would want?"

Since she was pretty sure they didn't sell Georgia moonshine on the ship, she opted to go with the light beer on tap he'd ordered last night, then turned back to her friend. "How much time do we have to loosen him up?"

Eyes closed, Michelle didn't look up. "Not much."

"I repeat Angie's question. What are we talking about?" Nancy took a sip of her new favorite drink.

"Shall we tell her?" Michelle teased.

Pam chuckled. "Sure"

"The next scheduled event is the Belly flop contest," Michelle announced, still comfortably soaking up the sun's rays.

"Is that all?" Angie asked, her head angled in Pam's direction.

"For now," Pam and Michelle echoed before bursting into giggles.

Angie shook her head, failing to hide her own laughter. "You guys need to be cut off."

"Lemonade here." Pam tilted her head in her friend's direction, wiggled her fingers in the air. "Remember?" With one eye open she spotted Kirk's approach. Time to shift the conversation, only her warning stilled on her lips when Michelle screeched loudly and shot upright. *Too late.* Kirk stood at his wife's side dripping cool pool water on her.

"Sorry." Kirk's unrepentant smile belied the apology. "Got a spare towel? The steward is out."

A large blue towel snapped in his direction. Laughing like a couple of frolicking teens, Kirk grabbed one end and curled his wife into his arms for a quick, drenching kiss.

Pam had to admit, when Michelle stumbled across that hunk, she did good. Very good. Once upon a time Pam had thought the same thing for herself. Thinking of which. She turned to glance in the direction of the pool. Rising out of the waters like a Norse God, Gil pushed off the edge of sky blue waters and stood perfectly still. Droplets glistening from the sun sprinkled across his shoulders, down his arms, his chest, and *oh my my*.

Hesitating a minute, he glanced from side to side as though only now realizing that he too would be needing a towel. Unless of course he planned to drip dry, and from the looks on some of the women currently entranced, not too many of them would object. And that bothered her more than it should have. Grabbing a nearby spare towel she'd kept handy in case she needed to cover up from the sun, she waved it in Gil's direction. The wide grin she received in response nearly stopped her heart. She was already having a hard time breathing at the site of him teetering on the pool's edge, now she had to remind herself to exhale. How after all these years could that man still so easily singe her from the inside out?

"Thanks." He grabbed the towel, their fingers barely touching, and the singe sparked.

"You're welcome," she actually managed to eek out the words as if she hadn't just forgotten how to breathe. He wiped his face dry and she almost cried when he draped the terry cloth around him.

"And now ladies and gentlemen," the speaker system blasted, "gather round poolside. In fifteen minutes we have the Great Belly Flop Challenge. All contestants can sign up with Harry by the kiosk."

Michelle glanced at her husband, flashed a hint of a smile, blinked, but didn't say a word.

"Oh, no." Kirk took a step back.

"Why not?" This time her smile inched higher to one side.

Gil chuckled under his breath, winked at Pam, then faced his new comrade in arms. "Good question. Why not?"

Slowly Kirk turned to face him. "You did hear the word Belly Flop?"

"I did."

"And if done right, it hurts like a son of a—"

"Shh," Michelle held her finger to her lips and tipped her head to the family with young children a few chairs down the aisle.

"No," Kirk continued. "But you can feel free to—"

"Sorry," Gil held up his hand. "I'm not the one with a wife batting her eyes at me."

"You can borrow mine." Kirk turned to Michelle and winked. "Bat your eyes. No man can resist you."

Michelle shook her head at her husband's bad joke. "I don't see why you don't want to try it. You guys didn't mind splashing half the passengers with your cannonballs."

Angie spit out a giggle, then slapped her hand over her mouth and mumbled, "sorry."

Until she'd done that Pam hadn't given any thought to the reference of cannons, balls, the husbands—or sort of husbands—in the same sentence.

"Of course," Michelle leaned back against the lounger, "you could do the event that comes after the line dancing. As a matter of fact, it might be fun for both of you."

Pam knew what was coming next and from the way Kirk's eyes studied his wife under crinkled brows, she had a feeling he was mentally going back in time through past cruises in search of the next possible event. Recollection had to have dawned when his brows shot up and he snapped his head from side to side. "Not happening."

"Party pooper." Michelle playfully puckered her lower lip.

Kirk secured his towel around his hips. "Let's take this back to the room and I'll show you party pooper."

The angelic side of Michelle's personality dipped her chin, pressed her lips tightly shut and blushed like a school girl at her husband's proposition.

"I remember those days." Nancy blew out a sigh and took another sip of her drink. "At least I think I do."

"I wish I did," Angie mumbled.

Gil turned to Pam, tightening the knot securing his towel, his blue eyes darkened to steel gray. The heat in his gaze said more to her than words ever could. Like her, he clearly remembered those days too.

Gil never should have let Kirk talk him into coming on deck with him. Aided by the need to update Pam on what he'd learned today, it had been too easy for his newfound friend to convince him to tag along after the handball game. The second Gil had laid eyes on his sort-of former wife sprawled out on the lounge chair, he knew his instinct to go back to his cabin, shower, change and catch up with Pam later in the day, preferably when she was fully clothed, would have been the better choice.

It was all he could do to stop from swallowing his tongue. Her red hair had darkened some through the years, but the deep shade of auburn suited her, as did the contrast with the royal blue swimsuit hugging her in all the right places. Detailed memories of every bend and curve of her shapely body flooded his mind. He couldn't wait to hit the cool swimming pool and get his thoughts back in line. And it had worked, until he'd returned to the group of friends and the playful banter. Keeping his cool had been an unexpected struggle. He wasn't a randy teen ruled by his hormones anymore. He was a grown man who had long ago learned to control his thoughts and testosterone impulses, not the other way around. But Nancy's innocent comment after the sexually heated exchange between Kirk and his wife had snapped the last thread of Gil's self-control. Heated days and nights from Georgia to Vegas and back flooded his mind with the force of an imploded dam. The best he could do was wrap himself in a towel and hope no one noticed his struggle. And for the most part, no one had. Except Pam. As sure of her thoughts as he was that there were four suits to a deck of cards, he'd have bet everything he owned, and then some, that Pam had been overwhelmed with the exact same memories.

"I should get back to my room and change," he said.

"Nonsense," Nancy chimed in. "Dry off here in the sun like the rest of us."

"Thanks, but I do have work to do."

A loud splat sounded in the background and the crowd that had gathered behind them roared. Angie straightened to peer between the people. "Sounds like the contest has started."

"Sure does," Michelle said with an air of disappointment.

Nancy eyed the two men from shoulder to shoulder, sighed, then finished the last sip of her drink. "What's up next?"

Kirk rolled his eyes and whispered to his wife, "How many of those has she had?"

Michelle held up three fingers and answered Nancy's questions. "Poolside games, but the gentlemen aren't cooperating."

"I really do have to work," Gil insisted over more cheers and splashes sounding behind them.

"All work and no play isn't good for a soul. Trust me I know." Nancy raised her glass and waved it at a waiter in the distance.

"Maybe you should take it easy on those?" Angie suggested softly.

"Nah, these things are just glori…fied milkshakes."

All gazes bounced from person to person, no one willing to insist Nancy be cut off. At least she wouldn't be driving.

"And ladies and gentlemen," the cruise director announced over the loud speaker as the calypso band picked at a few notes. "Stick around for our upcoming session of poolside line dancing."

"That's right!" Nancy sprang to her feet and grabbed Gil by the hand. "Come on big boy. You look like you've got lots of rhythm."

Pam's eyes widened, Michelle and Angie chuckled, and Gil didn't know which way to turn. What the heck had happened to the sourpuss woman from breakfast?

For a tipsy broad Nancy had a strong grip. "Let's show these people how it's done."

Before Gil knew what hit him, Nancy had yanked him in close, grabbed his other hand as well and began moving her feet in measured steps that he quickly realized was some form of swing dancing. In for a penny, in for a pound. He couldn't very well walk away. A spin here and a few twirls there, and a circle of passengers had formed around them. It had been years since he'd done any dancing. College actually. Climbing the corporate ladder didn't leave much time for clubbing, and Karen didn't care to cut a rug.

Ready to urge Nancy back to the group as the song came to an end, Gil slowed just as the band shifted tunes to something disco and Nancy clapped her hands, spun about, and grabbed hold of him once again. From over his shoulder he thought he heard Angie mumble something about moves.

There was no missing the low throaty rumble of Pam's laughter. From the corner of his eye he spotted her red hair and spun Nancy in the opposite direction just in time to hear Pam's voice. "Trust me his moves were never our problem."

# CHAPTER NINE

When Pam was growing up in rural Georgia there hadn't been a whole lot going on to entertain the county's teens. Probably the major contributor to half the youth of Porterville leaving town the moment they graduated high school. If not before. In the town diner, the old juke box hadn't gotten a new record since before Pam had been born. Probably because the diner, like the rest of the county, couldn't afford to keep up with progress or technology. She doubted there were many companies making new music for those rickety old tabletop boxes either.

Every once in a while when there were a few extra pennies to spend, but no where to go, some of the kids would wind up at the diner, push the few tables in the back to one side and do dance contests. The winner would get a free lunch from Gloria, the diner's owner. Free food was always great motivation to move your feet. She and Gil had become the couple to beat. Her father hadn't been worth a whole lot, but he had taught her to dance, which may have contributed to her A in that senior year dance class. Gil had taken the same class, and like everything else he did, he seemed to be a natural. The memory brought a smile to her face. He'd been a quick study and pretty soon was teaching her new moves, and not just on the dance floor.

"You're smiling an awful lot." Angie glanced momentarily at Pam before returning her attention to Nancy and Gil as well as the few couples who had paired up and joined them.

"I'm on vacation. I'm supposed to smile." No point in mentioning she'd just taken an unexpected trip down memory lane. Something she'd been doing a lot in the last twenty-four hours.

"Mm."

Tearing her gaze away from the couple dancing on deck, Pam faced her friend. "What does that mean?"

"Nothing." Angie kept her gaze on the dancers. "It just occurs to me that when you're with Leo your smile is different."

"What is that supposed to mean? Different?" Pam started to cross her arms, and decided instead to keep them at her side in a failing effort to feign casual and relaxed, and returned her attention to the dancers. "A smile is a smile."

"No. There are all sorts of smiles. The ones from *oh isn't that puppy cute* to *I've gotta secret* to *Tequila makes my clothes fall off*. With Leo I see puppies. With Gil, well…"

Pam was not taking the bait. Leo was good for her. Stable. Dependable. Kind. And Gil was…history. And marrying someone else. As soon as the divorce dilemma was sorted out.

"It strikes me," Angie rocked on the balls of her feet and back, "that fate could be trying to tell you something. Both of you."

"That's ridiculous. Gil will straighten everything out. You'll see. I'm getting married in St. Maarten."

"If you're sure."

She was. As attorney for the newspaper's owner, Leo had spent as much time in meetings with the owners and her boss as he had at his own place of business. They'd gotten along well enough, but one day his disposition darkened. She'd coaxed him into a cup of coffee in the cafeteria and slowly he'd shared his suspicions about his young wife. A few weeks and several cups of coffee later she'd learned the bimbo was stepping out with her yoga instructor. Leo might have forgiven her that, but the financial blow of using his money to pay for the lothario's studio remodel, added to the emotional blow of the betrayal, had been too much for even a nice guy like Leo to ignore.

Coffee chats became lunch, then dinner, soon they

added a movie or live performance, and somewhere between misery and friendship they concluded that best friends made the ideal spouses and falling in love was fleeting as well as highly over-rated. Companionship with benefits held much more appeal. She had no doubts. Until now.

"Here they come." Angie elbowed Pam.

"I was right." Nancy held her short hair up, exposing the nape of her neck to the fresh ocean breeze. "This man can move. We'll all have to take turns."

Angie swallowed a cough. At least this time she wasn't drinking anything she could spit out. Some days Angie had the sensibilities of a virginal teen. The girl needed a little corrupting.

The music started up again, this time to something more appropriate for a line dance. Considering how many people were on the boat, the number of folks who gathered together for the next activity seemed rather small.

"Now everybody. Follow me," the female member of the crew staff said into the mic. With her back to the crowd and in step with the beat of the music she clapped her hands and stepped left a few times, then right. There was more clapping, some heel clicking and finally spinning in place.

"We'd better get back to our seats before someone claims—" Before Pam could finish her sentence, another member of the crew staff came along and pulled her into the fray of line dancers.

Without thinking, she stretched her arm out and latched onto Gil's forearm, dragging him back to the dance area he'd just successfully escaped. The scene was choreographed chaos. For a few steps, everyone seemed to have the swing of it. Following the crew's lead, they slid left and left then right and right again. The entire group moved forward then back and finally swung around, shifting directions. By the third turn around they seemed to be getting the hang of it. The woman called out directions like a country band at a barn dance. People were laughing and giggling and every so often tipping sideways or stepping on someone's foot and laughing even harder.

Including Pam and Gil.

On the other side of the deck, near the loungers, Nancy took a long sip of water, her gaze pinned on the dancing passengers. "Those two seem to be having an awful lot of fun."

Keeping her eyes closed, Angie opted for shrugging her shoulder and wished Michelle and Kirk hadn't gone to their room to *change*. Had she realized that Pam and Gil were going to start getting cozy, she would have escaped to her cabin as well. Or perhaps now would be a good time to divide and conquer. "I'm getting hungry. Want to go check out the buffet?"

Nancy shook her head, and still staring, took another long swallow. Her gaze steady on Pam and Gil laughing like the high school sweethearts they once were, Nancy screwed the cap onto her bottled water. "I wonder just how close those two used to be?"

The woman picked one heck of a time to sober up.

Angie let out a resolved sigh. Next time she went on a honeymoon cruise she was going alone.

"There you are." George came up beside his wife. "How was trivia?"

"Didn't go."

A few steps behind him, Leo made his way through the passengers lingering about and came to a stop at Angie's side and smiled. "Enjoying the sun?"

Finally a question she could answer. "Loving it. No wonder people retire to Florida. Or buy an island."

Leo let out a rumbling laugh. "Know a lot of people buying islands, do you?"

"Not exactly." Angie smiled back at him. Leo always had a warm sense of humor. It was one of the things Pam enjoyed about him. *Pam.* Angie tossed her legs over the lounge chair and angled herself and Leo away from the line dancing session. "So, who beat the pants off of whom?"

"Cards were with Leo," George said over his shoulder before turning back to his wife. "I'm about ready for some food. How about you?"

"In a minute," Nancy answered, still watching the line

dancing.

As Angie had feared, everyone's gaze shifted to where Nancy was focused. George, bless him, didn't seem to notice a thing, he glanced and turned back to Nancy. "I'm starved. Shall we corral the others and get going?"

Leo, on the other hand, took a few seconds longer studying the dancing crowd. Though she hoped his eyes narrowed from the sun, Angie had a sneaking suspicion he'd spotted his fiancée and her unknown to him ex. Or was Leo actually starting to sniff out a stronger than explained connection? Either way, turning back to her, much to Angie's surprise, Leo was all smiles. "I say we corral the crew and indulge our appetites." He turned to Angie and extended a hand to her. "But first, shall we show them how it's done?"

# CHAPTER TEN

The elevator doors opened, and Gil stepped onto his floor. Between handball and dancing he'd gotten more of a workout than he'd had in years. And had a heck of a lot more fun too. He couldn't remember laughing so much in a very long time. His heart and blood still pumped hard and fast. His cheeks actually hurt from smiling. For a few minutes the years had slipped away and he was back in a time and place where life was good. Very good.

For too many years he'd focused solely on building his career and setting the foundations for a better life. A good life. Somewhere along the way he'd forgotten about living. No. Not somewhere. He knew exactly the day he stopped mixing life and living and used every minute of his day to get as far away from poverty-stricken Porterville, Georgia and everything it stood for.

*"Hello, Mr. Watson. Is Pam around?" Gil had had a crazy long week, getting settled into the dorms for the baseball team, setting up his schedule according to which teachers were partial to the sports programs and winning. He didn't bother explaining to the coach that he'd graduated from high school on the honor roll. His grades weren't high enough for an academic scholarship, but there was no doubt he had what it would take to graduate from college, even if the teachers weren't athlete friendly. Then there was actually registering for the classes, buying books, picking up equipment, attending long practices, following team imposed curfews and falling into bed sore, tired, and excited about doing it all over again. There'd been no time for phone calls. Except for a couple of calls from his mom*

*that had only set nerves on edge. Something didn't sound right. He was more than ready to hear Pam's voice. He needed to hear her voice.*

*"She's not here."*

*"Oh, well. What time will she be home?"*

*"She won't."*

*"What do you mean?" Something in Mr. Watson's voice had the hairs on the back of Gil's neck standing on end.*

*"She ain't living here no more."*

*Why hadn't she said anything to him? Had she found a job? Surely she would have tried to call for that. Left a message... Something. "Well, where is she living?"*

*"Don't know."*

*"What do you mean you don't know?" His mother had not been happy they'd run off together, and she'd been especially elated to learn that Pam would be willing to divorce if it would mean he could have enough scholarship money to attend the university as planned, but he'd always thought Mr. Watson had been okay with it all. Had believed in him. That some day he'd be able to provide a good life for Pam.*

*"She's moved on. Face it son, my Pammy isn't a one-man sort of woman. You'd best forget about her and get on with your life."*

The sound of laughter in the narrow hall snapped Gil back to the present, and he ignored the lingering shock of that miserable day. Walking hand in hand, laughing to themselves, occasionally bumping shoulders, Michelle and Kirk came from their suite.

"Hey man." Kirk nodded. "We're on our way to meet the gang for dinner. You joining us?"

Gil shook his head. "I need to get that shower. Take care of some business. You go on without me."

Michelle leaned into her husband. Not anything that he would call clingy, but just close enough to remain connected. If the sappy look on Kirk's face was any indication, he was all for connections. "Catch ya later."

As they walked away, Gil wondered how long those

two had been married. Even though they looked to be newlyweds, he'd heard enough from the conversation to know they were married and had a daughter. The way Kirk drank Michelle in with his eyes stayed with Gil as he opened his cabin door, crossed to the sliding glass balcony door and took a seat in the fresh air. He hadn't spoken with Karen since yesterday. There wasn't anything good to report, and he dreaded telling her that he'd need to stay on board for longer than he'd anticipated. He hated that he'd put Karen in this situation. She deserved better than that. An image of Kirk caressing his wife with his eyes flickered in Gil's mind. Karen deserved to be looked at the way Kirk looked at Michelle, like a man dying of thirst finally reaching his oasis.

And she deserved to know what was going on. He'd paid a small fortune for high speed internet and cellular usage, he might as well start collecting. Hitting two for Karen's number, he waited for the phone to pick up a signal. His muscles tightening with every unanswered ring.

"Hello."

"Hey. How's my favorite girl?"

"Hoping you'd call. Any more news?"

"I'm afraid so."

"Uh oh."

"One of the Buchanans was able to track down the problem. How doesn't matter now, but it's confirmed that the original papers were never filed."

After a long pause, his fiancée finally whispered, "Oh."

Karen was always on the move. Even when taking a call, she'd often get up and pace the floor while talking. He imagined for this news she'd sat down.

"Now what?" she asked.

"Caribbean divorce."

"Is there time?"

"All we need is four hours and as long as both of us show up in person, the Dominican courts will issue the final decree right away."

"And if only one of you goes?"

"Twenty-one days."

"Ouch." He could hear her controlled breathing even through the crappy connection. "Any idea what we'll tell Father?"

"I've already shot him an email stating a family emergency, but that I'd do my best to keep up online."

"This certainly does count as an emergency."

"And we are family." Or will be. That thought brought the only sliver of calm in the last forty-eight hours. Not that he was looking forward to being Allister Smythe's son-in-law so much. It was time. The grand bachelor life had grown old a long time ago. For some time now his eighty-hour work weeks had him longing for someone to come home to. *Someone.* Pam's face laughing as she tripped over the woman beside her with two, maybe three, left feet came easily to mind. That couldn't be good.

"You still with me?"

"Oh, yeah. Sorry. My mind is doing a lot of wandering these days."

"I know what you mean," Karen trailed off. She didn't sound quite like herself, but then again, faced with a mess like this, who would?

In the distance another cruise line sailed along. To him nothing more than a dot on the horizon, even though it was probably as massive a vessel as the one he was on, brimming with thousands of people having fun and making every effort to leave their reality behind at least for a few days. "I should have followed up. Asked for my copy of the decree rather than assume all had gone through."

"It's not your fault. You were young. Not everything in life can be neat and easy."

"Still. You deserve better than this." Better than him. *Him? Where had that thought come from?* From the lingering images of Kirk and Michelle. The man clearly adored his wife. And Karen most definitely deserved a man like that. Not to settle for her father's approval of a good match. He heard Karen's voice but his thoughts clouded the clarity of her words. "I'm sorry, what?"

"I said. So do you."

He pushed to his feet and rested his forearm on the rail.

He'd had adoration once. Or thought he had. Despite the love struck McEntires, Gil didn't believe in that kind of love anymore. Not one that would last. But Karen deserved to at least know what it felt like. She was a great woman. Despite the pre-ordained socialite life her father had created for her, she still stood her ground enough to become a respected broker in her own right. She could run her father's company with one hand tied behind her back. She didn't need Gil or any man, no matter what her father thought. Like himself, she'd focused her world on being the best. Together she and Gil had carried the business to heights even her father hadn't imagined. They'd made a great business team. It was only logical to see that team cross over into their personal lives. Her father never hesitated to point out marriage was after all nothing more than teamwork. He'd pushed and prodded, reasoned and rationalized until both he and Karen had come to agree they'd be good together. Marriage was the logical next step. Keeping the business all in the family. Neither was looking for starlight and symphonies. But still…

"Did I lose you again? Are you there?"

"Yeah. The connections in the middle of the nowhere are less than stellar."

"When will you be back?"

"I'll come back to the ship after the paperwork is done. No sense dragging my bags all over Hispaniola." He couldn't bring himself to admit he'd feel better knowing Pam had made the two-hour trip back to the ship safely. "I'll make arrangements too disembark and fly home from the next port the following day. That will give us a week to deal with whatever last minute crisis your parents come up with."

"After this little hiccup, whatever they come up with now won't even be a blip on my radar."

He chuckled. "No. I suppose not."

"It's going to be all right." Karen's voice faltered from her normal strong sure tone. "Isn't it?"

"Yes. We'll be fine." Whatever the heck *fine* meant. Right now he didn't know if anything would ever be the same again. Or if that was even what he wanted.

Famished, George insisted they bypass the sit down restaurant and head for the ready to eat buffet. Pam had to admit he had a point. She'd been enjoying herself so much, she hadn't noticed just how hungry she'd gotten until she saw all the food spread out like a king's feast. The dessert area had so many options she seriously considered skipping food and going straight to the coconut cream pie.

Seated beside her fiancé, she took a quick glance around the large eating area looking for Gil. Before George had whisked everyone away in search of food, Gil had leaned in and whispered to meet him after dinner at the front of the ship on the walking track. He didn't need to say why. It was obvious to any idiot he had news for her and despite the smiles and flush of exercise, had it been good news he would have said something, anything, right then. Even though she knew he wasn't coming, she looked anyhow. Just like that summer. She knew he was more than busy, but she'd waited and hoped his mother was wrong just the same until she couldn't stand it anymore. But that was a very long time ago. Water under the bridge as they say.

"You look way too pensive for a beautiful woman on vacation." Leo let his hand cover hers and squeezed.

He was such a nice guy. "Just debating what to choose for dessert."

"Have them all."

"Not if I want to fit into my wedding dress." She did her best to offer a relaxed smile, but something about the way Leo studied her didn't feel right. "Now who's the pensive one?"

Smiling back at her, he squeezed her hand before letting go. "Thinking about dessert."

Somehow Pam feared they were both thinking about the same thing. And it had nothing to do with coconut cream pie.

# CHAPTER ELEVEN

An ocean view as far as the eyes could see, and the breeze blowing in Gil's face, was the most relaxing experience he'd allowed himself to indulge in for what seemed like forever. Moving to the head of the line at Investco hadn't allowed much time, or opportunity, for relaxation.

"Have you been waiting long?"

At the sound of the familiar voice, Gil turned to see Pam come to a stop beside him. Her hair held back in a clip, the wind blew the ends in her face and pressed her brightly colored floor length sundress against the curves he was once very familiar with. "Not very."

"So." Moving into the space beside him, she leaned on the rail. "What's the scoop?"

"Still want to get straight to the punch line."

"Dancing around is only fun with music."

He bobbed his head. "An incompetent legal assistant failed to file."

Pam sucked in a sigh. "So we're still married?"

"Yes." He resisted the urge to reach out and grab her hand. Just to be sure, he stuck his hands in his pocket.

"Is there a solution?"

"Caribbean divorce. In Santo Domingo."

Pam shifted to face him fully. "We don't dock in Santo Domingo."

"No, but we do dock two hours away the day before St. Maarten."

She spun around again toward the view. "That's cutting it pretty close."

"It will be tight. But we can do it."

"We?" Pam tilted her head to look at him.

He nodded. "The only way to get a same day divorce is if we both appear."

"Oh, hell." She palmed her temple and rubbed in a steady circular motion.

Seeing Pam tangled up by frustration, Gil would need more than pockets to keep his hands still. Taking two steps to the side, he stood behind his former—in theory—wife and slowly lifted, then eased his hands onto her shoulders and began kneading away the tension. "You're going to have to tell Leo what's going on."

"Oh, I'm sure that's going to go over really well. *By the way dear, I'm still married. To my first husband. Hope you don't care that I've committed bigamy three times.* Which I've sort of neglected to mention."

Gil's hands stilled, "Mention what?"

Her spine stiffened. "He knows I'm divorced, but I may not have made a point of how many times."

Pam had always been good at confrontation, but light on disclosure. Which might explain why one day she was in Porterville and one day she was gone. Water under the bridge. He resumed measured pressure on her shoulders. "You need to tell him something."

"Not if we pull this off."

"It's up to you. But if it makes any difference, at least you're not a bigamist *now*."

Beneath his fingers, her shoulders tightened and he wished he'd said just about anything else.

She continued to look ahead. "I don't suppose you know the statute of limitations on that one?"

"You'll be happy to know there is no need for a statute of limitations. The crime ceases to exist once the simultaneous marriage is voided. Assuming your other divorces are legal, you're in the clear."

On a sigh, her head lolled back. "You would have to have added *if* the divorces were legal."

"Did you receive final divorce decrees?" He pushed harder on the tightened muscle cords in her neck.

Giving into the relaxing ministrations, her head rolled

forward again. "Yeah. I got smarter in my old age."

"You're not old."

"I'm not young."

"You are to me."

Pam lifted her head and turned to glance over her shoulder at him. "That's one of the nicest things I've heard in a long time."

"It's true. You're as beautiful as you were on the basketball court sophomore year."

"Sophomore year?" Pam spun around and Gil dropped his hands to his side.

He shrugged. "When you made the cheerleading squad."

"You remember that?"

"How could I forget? You were the most beautiful girl in the entire school. Took me two years to get up the nerve to ask you out."

"What?" Pam's mouth fell open in surprise and Gil's gaze dropped from her sparkling blue eyes to the full lips he still remembered and desperately wanted to taste.

"I, uh…didn't think you'd be interested in a geeky nobody."

Her gaze softened and her fingertips brushed lightly along his chin. "You were the kindest, smartest, hottest guy I'd ever met. You defended the bullied, tutored the struggling, and while you were at it, took the baseball team to the state championship two years in a row. I was over the moon when you noticed me."

The light fruity scent of Pam's perfume tickled his nose and his memory. "Elizabeth Arden Red Door."

"You remember."

"I remember everything about you." If he were offered his own kingdom, he couldn't tell you who closed the last gap, but there was nothing between them now. No air, no space, only warm soft lips and an overwhelming need for so much more.

Oh Lord. What had she done? Fire like this was only supposed to burn in the very young and hormonal, not a woman of her age and experience. And not from one kiss. Gil's fingers splayed across her back fueling desire like a fan to a flame. Cupping the back of his head she pulled him closer. Deeper. Everything felt so right. The heat, the warmth, the taste of him, the touch of him. Gil. So right. Her Gil. So... *wrong.*

Stung by the cool slap of reality, Pam sprang back. None of this made any sense. They'd moved on. She'd moved on. He'd moved on. They were marrying other people. Soon.

Arms at his side, Gil retreated an additional step. The heat lingering in his gaze almost had her falling back into his embrace.

She swallowed hard. "I—"

"I'—" his words tumbled over hers.

"We..." they both started again.

"That can't happen again," Pam finally spit out.

All Gil did was nod.

"I told Leo I was going to rest before we meet for miniature golf. I don't want to have lied."

Gil bobbed his head again. "I'll let you know when I hear more about Santo Domingo."

This time she dipped her chin in agreement. "I need to go." Before she did something stupid like throw herself at her *husband's* feet and beg him to change the world. Her world.

"I don't know." Michelle leaned back on the small sofa. "For two people who thought they were divorced, there seems to be an awful lot of energy passing between them."

"Energy?" That wasn't quite the word Angie would have used to describe the sizzle crackling under the surface whenever Pam and her ex were near each other.

"Did you hear Nancy's comments? She seems to have

noticed too."

"Only when she's sober."

"Doubt we're going to be able to keep her liquored up twenty-four seven."

Angie's lips pulled back in an exaggerated grin. "We could certainly try."

"Let's leave that for plan C."

"What's plan A and B?"

"I'm still working on those." Shaking her head, Michelle rubbed her hands together. "I wish Pam would hurry up. I'd like to know what to expect next."

"Oh you are an optimist." Angie stopped rearranging the hole in the wall known as a closet. "She should be back soo—"

The cabin door opened and Pam walked in. At the sight of both her friends waiting for her she plastered on a bright grin and developed a spring in her step. "Well. The not so good news is that we are most definitely still married."

"Oh boy," Michelle muttered.

"The better news is that it looks like we can get a same day divorce in Santo Domingo the day before we dock in St. Maarten."

"Oh boy," Angie echoed Michelle's sentiments.

"But the better news—"

"Good. I think we could use some better news." Michelle shifted to the edge of her seat.

"I can't be arrested for bigamy over any of my previous husbands."

Michelle flopped back on the sofa again. "No. Only for the next one if this same day divorce doesn't work."

"Pam," Angie took a seat beside Michelle and folded her hands in front of her. "Does this mean you're going to tell Leo who Gil is?"

Pam shook her head. "I still say there's no reason for him to find out there was a glitch in a long ago divorce. Once the glitch is fixed all will be as it should."

"And if the glitch can't be fixed?"

"It can. And it will."

"Now who's the optimist? What does Gil say about all

this?" Michelle asked.

From the way the color momentarily flushed to Pam's cheeks, Angie knew there was most definitely something her friend was not telling them. "Uh oh. You'd better spill."

"There's nothing more to tell."

"Oh, yes there is. I can see it in your eyes. You're holding back on us."

Michelle stood and circled her friend, eyeing her carefully. "Slight whiff of unfamiliar man's cologne."

"There are a lot of men on this ship," Pam answered.

"Your cheeks are flushing," Michelle added.

"It's the Caribbean. It's warm here."

"Thermostat is set to seventy," Angie joined in. "Try again."

Michelle circled her one more time, her hand outstretched as though about to grasp some forensic evidence.

"Oh, all right," Pam snapped, sidestepping her friend. "We may have kissed."

"Uh oh." Michelle dropped into the nearest chair. "You're still in love with him."

# CHAPTER TWELVE

Standing dockside in Nassau, Pam pretended not to notice her ex-husband. As far as she was concerned the perfect scenario for the next week would have been for Gil to stay cloistered in his cabin. Out of sight out of mind. *Right.* And Lucille Ball was a natural redhead. Not that it mattered.

Just her luck, Leo had as much in common with Gil as his own shadow. Since Gil hadn't joined the group for dinner, nor later at the after supper club, Leo went to his cabin and escorted him up to join them. At first it hadn't been too bad as they sat off to the side talking shop, but by the end of the night, Leo had christened Gil part of the clan. Leo was too blasted friendly for his own good, and too darn persuasive. It hadn't taken long in their relationship for her to realize there was no point in arguing with a litigator. And Leo was one of the best.

None of this would be a problem if Gil had only grown paunch and grouchy—and weren't still such a heart-stopping kisser. For those few seconds on deck she'd been swept back in time. The sensations and memories sluicing over her like a warm shower after a hard day. Even now, the next day, it took a conscious effort to keep her fingers from brushing across her lips. Whether to mitigate the heat the mere memory sent coursing through her or seal the sensations a while longer, she wasn't sure. What she did know was that she couldn't still have feelings for Gil. Too many years had passed. So much had changed.

Despite her friends' insistence, she'd sworn up and down that she was not still in love with Gil Harris. She couldn't be. She hardly knew the man he'd become. But that didn't mean her hormones weren't on high alert whenever he came near. The guy had to have enough pheromones to attract most of the women in the western hemisphere. If Gil and she had remained married she would have probably spent all these years beating ladies off with a stick.

And from the looks of things, whether she liked it or not, she was going to have to get used to spending this trip with her past, turned current, and future husbands. Just what every woman wanted—a honeymoon for three.

While Kirk and Leo bartered with the hansom cabbies over the price for an island tour group, Pam admired the handy work of some local artisan and pretended having Gil standing beside her didn't matter.

"Did you see this one?" Gil pointed to the shiniest shell on display.

The sparkly shell had caught her eye from across the way. "It's pretty."

"You still like sparkle, don't you?"

His remembering she liked all things that glittered shouldn't have meant so much, but it did. Swallowing the smile threatening to take over her face, she didn't trust her voice and opted for a simple nod.

Angie turned her attention from Leo and Kirk to the handmade jewelry. "You'd think these horse and buggy rides were a matter of life and death." Being the most easygoing of the crowd, Angie would have gladly paid the drivers whatever they'd asked. Not that she had money to burn, but like Pam, she appreciated how hard it was to earn a buck.

Nancy, sifting through keychains and other inexpensive gadgets with one eye while glancing over at Gil with the other, turned her attention to her husband. "I'm surprised you're not in on this."

"Nope. Big brother can take care of himself." George turned to Gil. "If you ask me, lunch at Señor Frog's would have been plenty of sightseeing. If you've seen one island, you've seen them all."

"And the inside of one seaside bar is like any other,"

Nancy responded, shaking her head. The stone-faced woman was making another appearance.

Gil smiled and shrugged, and drew his gaze away from the trinkets Pam was pretending to admire. He made her wonder if he wouldn't have preferred to spend the day anywhere else as well.

"Okay. We've got the two buggies." Beaming, Leo gave Pam a quick peck on the cheek. "The four of us will take one cab." His hand circled from Angie and Gil to himself and Pam. "And you four," he pointed to his brother and Kirk, and their wives, "will have the other. If we get separated for any reason, we'll meet at the Frogs for lunch."

Pam didn't dare do more than smile and start walking. Gil was simply too close for comfort. Reaching the first wagon, Angie stepped up to the back row of seating and prepared to climb up.

"Here," Leo hurried to catch up to the girls and extended his hand. "Let me help you."

"Thanks, Leo. Always such a gentleman, but I think I got this."

Leo nodded but didn't let go.

Anxious to take her seat and do her best to practice that out of sight out of mind idea, Pam grabbed the metal brace on one side and hoisted herself up and then she proceeded to very ungracefully slip and fall backwards.

"Whoa." Gil lurched forward in time to grab hold of her waist. "You okay?"

Pam nodded. "Just clumsy," she breathed. Blast if this man's touch was going to be the end of her.

Gil's grip at her side held on a moment longer than he should have, but she finally leveraged herself forward again, and he eased back and waited until she was settled before he stepped back.

"Thanks," Leo passed in front of him. "Precious cargo."

Gil nodded and took the seat beside Angie. First thing after only a short distance, the cabbie insisted they stop at the bottom of the Queens's staircase and walk up the 66 steps to an old fort and that he would pick them up at the top.

She was first to the top, when she turned, Gil was only a few steps behind. Leo had slowed to take a few photographs with Angie waiting behind him.

"He seems like a really nice fellow." Gil shifted his stance, watching her fiancé below.

"That's probably because he is." Too nice a guy to find himself with a fiancée who already had a husband.

Turning slowly about, Gil took in a deep breath. "I really need to remind myself to do this more often."

Pam chuckled. "Track down wives?"

One side of his mouth tipped up in a slow grin. "Take a break. Enjoy the fresh air."

"You work too hard don't you?"

He shrugged. "I don't know about too hard…"

Something in his eyes reminded her of Kirk when he first came to the paper. A man driven by his career. She crossed her arms and leaned against an ancient pony wall. "Want to try that again."

This time his smile widened. "Okay, maybe a little hard."

Eyes that twinkled with amusement were one of the many things she'd loved about this man. Being the window of the soul and all that. Not that it mattered any more. "It's not good for you."

"No. no it's not." His expression turned serious and Leo made it to the top before she could say anything else.

It didn't take long to stroll across the historic site. When the buggy came up the road, she was torn between wanting to learn more about the man Gil had become and rushing back to the boat, tucking all memories of him back where they belonged in an old memory.

The group moved on, trotting along through the small town of tourist shops, into the residential neighborhoods with colorful homes. The cabbie did most of the talking, explaining the history and importance of all the different buildings and homes. As hard as she tried to pay attention, her thoughts muddled back and forth between memories of twinkling eyes and reminding herself just how long ago and faraway Gil belonged.

The person who seemed to be enjoying the tour the most was Angie having a blast people watching.

"So where do you think those two are from?" Angie pointed discreetly to an older couple, the man in Bermuda shorts, white socks and brown sandals. The woman in a bright floral dress wore a basket weave hat with a wide blue ribbon. All the hat needed was plastic fruit and it would have matched the bonnet on the head of the horse in front of them.

"I vote Florida," Pam said with a forced smile. How much trouble could she get into chatting about tourists with her friend. "Typical snowbirds."

"And those," Angie pointed to a younger couple, "holding hands. I vote honeymooners."

Pam nodded. "Could just be away from the children and thrilled to be playing adult."

"Maybe," Angie nodded.

"I'm with Pam," Gil chimed in.

Angie smiled. "Why?"

"Just a hunch. If they were honeymooners they'd be walking closer together, touching more. Besides, when they stopped to look in that window, she swayed in place."

"Makes sense." Leo dipped his chin a few times.

"I'm missing something." Angie inched forward in the chair.

"Second honeymoon," Gil explained. "Child is probably a toddler or younger because mom's still used to rocking from holding the baby."

Angie sat back, slightly slack jawed, and looked at Gil. "Do you have kids?"

"Nope."

Pam glanced behind her, her gaze momentarily locking with Gil's. She hadn't had a chance to sit and talk. Ask about his life.

"But," he continued, "I have two sisters who did the same thing."

"I have two boys, grown. My first wife passed right after the youngest graduated college." Leo turned to face Gil again. "You been married before?"

Pam tensed in her seat, her grip tightening on her purse

strap.

"Once," Gil answered. "Youthful indiscretion."

Pam closed her eyes and drew in a slow calming breath. Indiscretion. She's been an indiscretion.

"How did it take so long for a gal to snag a smart young man like you?"

Even though she could feel Gil's eyes boring into her back, she refused to turn around and look.

"I've been asking myself the same question lately."

"Oh, look," her voice a little shrill, Angie interrupted with a bit more enthusiasm and urgency than normally required. "We're back dockside. Time for Senor Frogs."

Bless her. Pam was going to owe a lot of people big time when this trip was over. Assuming she survived.

"So what is it you do exactly?" Nancy skewered Gil with a questioning glare.

"He told you honey," her husband George answered. "Investment Broker."

Gil took a sip of his beer and debated which way to turn. Too many inquisitive people and he didn't dare look in Pam's direction. Every time he did, another memory of their time together floated to the surface. He was beginning to feel like a shipwreck survivor surrounded by flotsam in need of a life raft.

"Oh yeah," Nancy bit down on a tortilla chip, but kept her gaze on Gil. "You did, didn't you?"

He wished she weren't so darn interested in him. The way she'd stared at him last night and again today made him more than uncomfortable, and that was never a good thing.

"This guacamole is just wonderful." Angie stabbed at the green dip. "I wonder if we can have an order to go?"

"I don't think you're allowed to bring food onto the ship." Leo reached for another chicken wing. "Health concerns."

"I don't know." Nancy looked around, "These folks look pretty healthy to me."

Everyone at the table chuckled and slowly the conversation shifted to plans for the rest of the afternoon. Nancy had become a sun worshipper. Though Gil suspected the frozen drinks held way more appeal to her than the sun. He wasn't one to encourage imbibing to excess, but the more alcohol she consumed, the less interest she directed at him and that idea sat just fine with him.

George, on the other hand, was still eager to try out the bingo machines, and Leo seemed determined to gather a full table of poker players. When the conversation turned again, this time towards plans for tomorrow and the next island, Gil begged off, "Seriously guys, I know you'll have a lot of fun, but I do have to get some more work done."

"Mm," Nancy hummed.

"The ship has a tour of the churches I'd like to take." Angie reached for another chip. "Anyone care to tag along?"

"You know," Leo pulled out his cell phone. "You can probably find a cheaper tour online."

"Yeah," Kirk faced Leo, "but then she runs the risk of being left behind if there's a mishap like a vehicle breakdown. If she's part of an official tour the ship has to wait for the passengers no matter how delayed or what reason."

"Unless she leaves her kid behind." Michelle chuckled and all eyes turned to her. "Well, that is if she had any."

"Did somebody really leave their child behind?" Angie asked.

Michelle nodded. "Sort of. On my first cruise, we were all aboard, the horns sounded and the ship pulled away from the dock. About twenty minutes later we came to a full stop. Everyone noticed and started speculating as to what the heck was going on. People were coming up with all sorts of crazy stories from the plausible medical emergency to the absurd, hijacked by pirates."

"In the Caribbean?" Nancy asked. Gil was pretty sure her husband mumbled something about Pirates of the

Caribbean under his breath, but the rest of the table held their tongues.

"The captain," Michelle continued, "finally came on the loud speaker and explained that they'd gotten a call form the company's sister ship still in port informing him that a couple from our ship had been left behind. He continued to explain that normally he would not hold the ship, but this time he could not in good conscience leave these people behind since their ten-year old daughter was on board."

"Oh, dear," a voice muttered.

Angie's next mouthful stopped midway to her mouth. "How the heck did that happen?"

"The kid wanted to do a different land package than her mom and dad," Kirk interjected. "One of the other parents said the daughter could go with them and their family."

"And the moral of the story is," Michelle continued, "unless you plan to leave your child behind as collateral, pay for the ship's tours."

The group chuckled, and Leo tipped his glass toward his fiancée. "Agreed."

Though Gil raised his glass, the little story left him pondering with how chummy everyone had become, how the heck were he and Pam going to escape this crowd for an entire day when the ship arrived on Hispaniola? Or worse, how in heaven's name was she going to explain to her loving fiancé if, like the wayward parents, they too missed the last call to board?

# CHAPTER THIRTEEN

Over the better part of the last few days Gil had managed to spend limited time with Pam's entourage, but he could only push his luck so far. The cruise lines private island port held a little bit of something for everyone and Gil figured a small beach with a few thousand people mulling about was probably the safest setting in which to be near Pam.

The ship's tender pulled into the slip and disembarking took considerably less time than embarking. Leo and Pam led the way. Gil hung back behind the crowd.

"You sure you don't want to join us?" Kirk asked over his shoulder.

"Not this time, thanks." Landlocked most of his adult life, Gil had never gotten the chance to try parasailing. Though he had to admit the call to adventure had him itching to say *hell yes,* but the fear of breaking his neck and winding up in intensive care instead of a Santo Domingo courtroom tomorrow kept him from doing anything too adventurous. Or crazy. He would however make it a point to convince Karen they needed to make time to travel more. He'd put away his daredevil antics the day he graduated school, and after a week on this floating never never land, he'd begun to realize that he definitely needed to take more time to enjoy living.

"Have it your way," Kirk squeezed his wife's shoulder and a few minutes later, they were onboard a nearby boat and gearing up.

"They're nuts if you ask me." Pam stood staring at the couple in the nearby slip. "I love those two. Really I do. But given the chance they can be a little crazy."

Gil laughed. "Crazy must be good. They look very happy."

"They are. Classic case of opposites attract and form the perfect balance."

"How is that?"

"Michelle used to be very subdued, proper. The word librarian comes to mind."

"Really?" He glanced back at the woman in a stunning bikini, laughing and joking with the man at her side. "Hard to believe. Which means Kirk was—"

"Adrenaline on steroids. The guy looked like he'd fallen off the cover of GQ magazine. A special playboy edition."

"And he fell in love with the librarian." Almost the reverse of him and Pam. She'd been the madcap, daredevil. The girl who was up for anything. He'd been the quiet, smart kid. Making an effort to be seen and noticed by her had been the surprise catalyst to uncovering a hidden talent. He could throw a ninety mile an hour fast ball and hit the catcher in the breadbasket every time. Didn't matter that he couldn't bat worth a damn or outrun a ball. He could pitch both lefty and righty and never flinched under pressure. By junior year the college scouts were beating down his door. It had become his ticket out of Porterville, thanks to Pam.

Leo strolled up behind them. "The scuba lessons are almost sold out. I grabbed the last three spots."

"Three?" Pam spoke up first. "I thought you and Angie were the only two who wanted lessons?"

For the first time, Gil saw Leo's mantle of authority slip. The guy's gaze shifted to the water and back. "I thought once we hit the beach you'd change your mind."

Gil coughed with suppressed laughter. "That'll be the day."

Pam whirled around and glared at him.

"Sorry," he hefted an apologetic shoulder. "But you were always one to keep a safe distance from the water. I can't picture you in the water, never mind under it."

Not till Angie's gaze skipped nervously from Gil to a suddenly studious Leo did Gil consider he may have revealed a tad too much understanding for *old friends*.

Hands fisted on her hips, Pam turned on Leo. "I see no reason to ruin a perfectly good vacation by drowning."

Hesitating a beat too long before hiding his thoughts behind a broad smile, Leo turned to Pam and chuckled. "You won't drown."

"There might be room on the glass bottom boat with Nancy and George." Angie redirected everyone's attention to Leo's niece and nephew. "Maybe one of you two would like to scuba?"

Brent shook his head. "Sis and I are going kayaking."

"Oh no." Emily lifted her hands in defensive mode and shook her head at her brother. "The last thing I want is to go kayaking with my brother. He'll dump me on my rear and think it's hilarious."

"I will not." Brent chuckled and Gil found himself agreeing with Emily. From the gleam in Brent's eyes, the kid would totally laugh his butt off if he knocked his sister into the water.

"Maybe Brent and I can give kayaking a whirl." Gil patted Brent on the shoulder. He wouldn't mind hearing more about the guy's plans.

"And I will find a nice spot under a shady tree." Pam waved it the general direction of the shaded shoreline.

Leo moved closer, and Gil thought Leo's gaze flickered in his direction a second. "I don't like leaving you alone."

"Alone?" Pam chuckled and smiling shook her head. "Alone with two thousand people? I will be perfectly fine."

"I don't know." Leo pressed his lips tightly together. Gil had heard Leo and Angie gush over this particular excursion more than once. The ship offered lessons too, but Leo insisted he could do that in any pool in any city. He wanted the island experience. At first Angie hadn't seemed all that interested, but by this morning she was as excited as Leo. Personally, Gil would have been content with a little snorkeling.

"Please. Go." Pam let her hand fall on Leo's forearm. "Have fun. I'll wait here."

Reluctantly Leo agreed and with a young lady on either side, they followed the walkways to the other side of the cove.

"I'll go see about the kayaks. Be right back." Without giving Gil a chance to respond. Brent was off and running down the beach.

"It could be worse," Pam said watching her friends disappear in the distance.

"How's that?" Gil asked.

"He could have wanted to do the zip line."

Gil burst out laughing. "Now that sounds like my adventurous Pam. I can see you gliding across the shore."

One eyebrow shot up as she spun about to face him. "Seriously? You can see me strapped in a harness, smashing my hair under a protective helmet and—"

"Stop." Gil held up his hand, smiling. "What was I thinking?"

"That's better." Pam nodded, a lazy smile lifting one side of her mouth. A very kissable mouth.

He took a half step in retreat and smiled back. "Now if the helmet had glitter?"

Pam's smile bloomed into a full fledged grin. "Maybe."

The urge to press his lips to that adorable smile almost had him forgetting who they were and why they were here together after all these years. "Let's find you a chair before all the good places are taken."

"But Brent—"

"Will find me." To nudge her along, he put his hand to the small of her back, quickly regretting the contact and sizzling undercurrent that followed. He'd thought the heat they'd shared had been a thing of youth. The reason why no other had woman affected him so hard and fast. But the first fissure appeared in that self-delusion the moment he first laid eyes on Pam, and shattered completely when a simple, brief kiss left him hot, bothered, and totally confused.

The way Pam sucked in a soft breath at his touch, he wondered if she was as taken aback as he was by the renewed contact. Stopping at the edge of the sandy beach, it took her a few seconds to scope out the best spot and point. "Over there."

"Okay." Casually waving an arm at a cluster of lounging tourists, she looked worthy of a master's sculpture. What he needed now was some distance before he made a total fool of himself. "You go stake your claim and I'll grab a couple of towels from the kiosk."

"And I'll keep an eye open for Brent."

"Deal." He trotted back to the area the ship had set up for passengers needing a beach towel. Breathing deeply, he distracted himself by taking a long look around. The cruise line had created quite a little island spread. Clearly only for the ship's passengers the courtyard was speckled with shops, vendors, tours, and the central attraction, a massive outdoor barbecue buffet. Already the food was being hauled in from the ship and the smell of grilling ribs was helping him forget a different hunger.

Two towels tucked under his arm, he made his way back to Pam. "Here you go."

The large palm tree she'd settled under offered a nice canopy of shade. Enough for several loungers.

"Thanks." Pam stretched out her hand and it took Gil a few seconds to remember what he was doing. She'd taken off the psychedelic tunic she'd had on and was wearing a neon pink two-piece bathing suit.

The sight sucked all the saliva from his mouth and had him struggling for air. This was crazy. "Need anything else?"

"Nope." She flashed a quick smile then dove into her beach bag coming back up with a massive tube of sunscreen. "Even in the shade I have to be careful."

"I remember." Lobster red was the first thought that came to mind. It had driven her nuts that she couldn't play at the lake or spend an afternoon on the bleachers watching his games like everyone else. She'd learned the hard way that she couldn't afford to miss a single spot when slathering on the sunscreen. "Better let me help."

"I've got it."

Tipping his head to one side, he rolled his eyes at her and waited for her to realize even the best of contortionists would nee help.

"Just my shoulders." She relented. "I won't roll over."

He nodded and accepted the tube. About to squirt it on

her shoulders he remembered the last time he'd done that. She'd shot five feet into the air, snatched the tube from him and squirted him from head to toe. They'd wrestled playfully over the last remnants of lotion and fallen into a laughing heap. That had been a very, very long time ago.

"You still there?"

"Sorry." He squirted the lotion onto his palms and then carefully and uniformly spread the warmed liquid across her shoulders. She still felt good.

A clearing throat sounded behind him and Gil turned to see Brent standing quietly.

Gil replaced the cap on the sunscreen and handed the tube back to Pam. "You should be safe from the mean sun."

"Thanks again."

"Any time." He probably shouldn't have said that, but he'd meant it. More than he should.

"Oh my word!"

The voice pulled Pam from a quiet, comforting cushion.

"Oh, Pam dear."

The concerned voice belonged to Leo. Forcing her eyes open she had to squint from the bright light. Not any light. Sunlight.

"How long have you been asleep?"

"Not very."

"Uh oh." That voice belonged to Angie.

"Ouch," the unfamiliar voice had to be Emily.

Sitting up, Pam winced at the unexpected pinch to her stomach, followed by a sharp twinge at her cleavage when she twisted to better look at Leo. "Oh no."

"Oh, yeah." Angie sighed. "You didn't move with the sun."

"No kidding," she muttered. She remembered reading her book and noticing the edge of shade barely covering her chair and thinking she'd have to move soon. Obviously she hadn't.

Leo inched forward to grab her arm and halfway between them thought better of it, dropping his hand to his side. "We'd better get you some first aid."

"No. Been here, done this, bought the aloe vera. I think I'll skip lunch and get back to the room. Take a cool shower and soak myself in more lotion."

"I don't know." Leo shook his head. "A lobster looks pale in comparison."

*Tell me something I don't know* was on the tip of her tongue, but no sense in being snarky to Leo. It wasn't his fault she'd fallen asleep in the sun and fried herself to a crisp. "I'll be fine."

"If you insist, but I'm walking you to your room."

Pam nodded and reached for her beach bag.

"I'll take that." Angie snatched it up before Pam could get close.

The idea of bending at the waist wasn't a good one right now. "Thanks."

"I smell food." George called from just ahead of them before noticing Pam's color. "Oh dear."

"Oh, honey," Nancy added.

"I'm taking her back to the ship." Leo ignored his family and kept walking.

"That's for the best." Nancy nodded. "We'll check in on you later."

Pam gave a queen's wave and kept moving. Of all the dumb things to do, two days before her dream wedding and the day before her divorce. Wasn't tomorrow going to be just peachy.

# CHAPTER FOURTEEN

"**N**ot bad for an old man."

"Not bad for a kid," Gil countered. The kayaking had been a blast and when they were done, Brent had challenged Gil to a windsurfing race. Fortunately for him no one he knew was around to record their efforts.

"I hope there's still some of that barbecue lunch left. I'm famished."

"I'm sure there's more than enough, but I doubt the others waited for us." Following the scent of cooking beef, Gil kept an eye out toward where Pam had been sunbathing.

"Look." Brent pointed ahead. "My folks are over there."

Nancy waved them over. "Grab a plate," she said when they were close enough to hear, "There's plenty."

Gil stayed on Brent's heels. "Does your family travel together like this often?"

"No. Mom decided we needed family time."

"Who screwed up?" Gil said half kidding, half serious.

Brent loaded his plate with ribs and shrugged. "That would be me."

Longing for the days when he could eat like a horse, Gil grabbed only a couple of ribs. "How bad?"

"To me, not bad at all. To my mother, the world is coming to an end."

Based on the plans Gil had heard, the kid wasn't talking jail time, so that left one thing. "A girl?"

Brent nodded and dumped a mound of potato salad on the already full plate.

"Want to tell me about it?" Gil skipped the potato and went for the mac and cheese. Still carb heavy but tastier.

"She's wonderful." The kid's face brightened. "Smart, sexy, happy. She brings out the best in me."

"But…"

"She's a waitress."

And George and Nancy were definitely not blue collar. "So now what?"

"Nothing."

"You're willing to give her up?"

"Hell no." Frowning, Brent turned a steely gaze on him. "I'm not twelve years old. My mother doesn't get to pick my friends. Or my wife."

"Wife." He was going to have to stop calling Brent kid. "Wedding plans after graduation?"

Brent didn't say a word. His only reaction was a tick along the edge of his jaw. Spoonful of baked beans mid air, whatever Gil had said, the kid, Brent, seemed to lose his yearning for more food and he set the spoon down.

And then it hit Gil with the force of a two-ton sledge hammer. "You're already married."

Brent flung around. "I didn't say that."

"You didn't have to, but you are. And your parents don't know. And now you have to choose?" Pot meet kettle.

"It's not like that. We didn't have to get married."

"And *I* didn't say *that*."

"No. No you didn't. That was the first thing Emily said when I told her."

"So your sister knows, but not your parents?"

"She won't rat me out. At the end of this year I'll have a good job and then we can tell my mother. But not as long as she controls the purse strings for tuition."

Some things never changed. "You could have waited until after graduation."

"Why?"

Gil looked at him. The two men now stood in the middle of the compound with plates full of food and no intention of moving. He didn't know how to answer the question. He hadn't waited until he graduated college to get married. But he couldn't hide his wife from a baseball team that easily, nor from the scholarship committees. "It might have been easier."

"Who said life was supposed to be easy?"

"How old are you again?"

Brent chuckled. "Twenty-one. Of sound mind and body. We're in love. If I love her enough to live with her then I should love her enough to marry her. And if I don't love her enough to marry her, I have no business wanting to live with her."

"And you love her enough." It wasn't a question.

His face lit up. "I can't imagine a single day of my life without her. It's sappy or corny or whatever you want to say, but it's true. No matter what happens in my day, I want that day to end with her. And I'm not giving her up."

"Even if your mother found out and pulled the plug on your funding?"

Brent's back stiffened as he sized up his opponent. "I wouldn't be much of a husband if I ran at the first sign of adversity, would I? I'd appreciate it if you'd keep this little conversation of ours in confidence."

Gil nodded and took an extra second to follow in the young man's footsteps. Not that he deserved to. How different would his life have been if he'd had the backbone to choose Pam over some stupid scholarship?

"Well, at least this solves the problem of tomorrow." Angie hung her wet swimsuit in the shower.

"And how is that?" Flat on her back, Pam hadn't done much thinking about anything other than how to get Leo to stop hovering over her like an Italian grandma.

"Tonight at dinner Kirk, Michelle, and I will convince Leo to join us on the all day excursion instead of the one he's been talking about."

"Right." Pam sighed. "And all I have to do is find..." Brilliance suddenly dawning, she sprang up, ignoring the bite of her skin. "And now I have a good reason to stay behind."

"Bingo." Angie tapped her nose. "Give the lady a prize."

"It will be a little dicey, getting back before everyone. I may need you guys to cover for me some if we're delayed, but I think it should work."

"Especially since you sent Leo packing, claiming the best cure was to leave you alone with a cool sheet and quiet."

"Which, unfortunately, is the truth. Clothes hurt." Even the seams of the t-shirt she had on scratched at her shoulders.

A soft rap on the door broke the conversation.

"If that's Leo again," Pam pushed to her feet and swallowed a groan from the painful movement of skin against skin, "I might just throw him overboard."

"Those are pretty strong emotions from a woman who keeps marrying men like her first husband."

Half way to the door, Pam spun around. "What!"

"Think about it. What was your last husband?"

"An engineer."

"He was also," Angie counted off on her fingers, "strong, smart, determined—"

"Better hurry up and make your point."

"So is Leo. He's a strong, smart, and determined lawyer."

Pam shook her head and continued on her path to the door.

"And so is Gil," Angie said to Pam's back. "It looks to me like everyone else has been a rather poor imitation."

Ignoring the absurd observation, Pam bit down on her back teeth and flung the door open prepared to give her smart and determined fiancé the lecture of his life about letting her rest in peace. "I told you all I need…"

Gil stood on the other side of the door, a large blue jar in his hand. "Is this?"

Squinting at the jar in an effort to read the label, Pam stammered an apology, "I thought you were, I mean… I'm sorry. What is that?"

"George and Nancy filled us in on the burn when Brent

and I got back to the barbecue." He held up the jar. "It's massage cream. Had to offer to buy you and Leo a his-and-her massage as soon as you recover, and then swear on my mother's grave I wouldn't tell a soul the spa manager sold me this while we're still docked."

Pam stared at the jar. Maybe her first strong and determined husband was also a little crazy.

"Stop looking at me like that. It's better than aloe vera for sunburn. Seals moisture in. Eases the pain." He held it up along with a large wad of fabric. "I hope you don't mind, since the shops are completely closed up while we're in port, I brought you one of mine. It's the longest T-shirt I have."

"Thank you." It occurred to her that when Angie described Pam's first husband she neglected to include charming, considerate, and incredibly thoughtful.

"Excuse me." Angie edged past Pam. "Since we skipped the barbecue, while he's here to keep you company, I'm going to run upstairs and get a tray of lunch. I'll bring you back something too." She cast a quick glance from Pam to Gil then back to her friend again before scurrying out the open door. Several steps down the hall, Angie called over her shoulder, "I'll take my time."

Gil squinted after her friend. "What was that all about?"

"Nothing. She's delusional." Or insightful. For her own sanity, Pam was going with the former. She took the cream from him. "Thank you."

"You should put that on right away. And layer it thick."

"The voice of experience?"

He shrugged. "Spring break. Waterskiing at a friend's lake house. All day on the water. No sunscreen. My shoulders looked like yours."

Pam eased away from the door. "This is crazy. I didn't realize how many creases the human body has. When I walk the front of my ankles hurt. When I bend, my stomach hurts. If I try and lay sideways my cleavage hurts. Thank God my back is okay or I'd be even more miserable."

"There's something worse than miserable?" Gil smiled and Pam resisted the urge to smack him. "Let me at least put this on your ankles so you don't have to bend so far. Angie can help you with the rest."

"That won't be necessary. I can reach my own ankles."

"Okay." He nodded, pulling out the vanity chair. "Go ahead. I'll just rest here a minute before going back to my room."

"That won't be…"

Before she could finish her sentence, he installed himself on the seat and crossed his arms.

"Oh, very well." Slowly she eased herself onto the bed, careful to keep her back straight and not bend at her tummy.

Gil raised a single brow, but didn't say a word.

Taking her time, Pam unscrewed the cap and scooping out a dab, rubbed it between her thumb and forefinger. It was much thicker than any of the lotions she and Angie had brought with them. Digging out a little more, she gritted her teeth at the tendril of pain shooting up her arm from the crease of her elbow and rubbed it onto her other forearm.

"Don't rub it in. Leave it on. Like a paste. That's why I brought you the t-shirt, so you don't get the sheets all dirty."

Pam squinted at her arm. Even rubbing it in she felt better, but the thought of bending her arm once again to redo the application had her sucking in a fortifying breath. She could do this. She had to do this.

"Here." He stood and crossed the small room in two long strides. "Let me show you."

On one knee he picked up her foot, careful not to bend her leg, he dipped his fingers into the jar and pulled out a solid clump. With a painstaking tenderness, he wiped it across the top of her foot and along the sides to just above her ankle.

Right about now she couldn't say if she felt better because of the cream or his touch.

"Shall I do the other foot?"

Pam bobbed her head.

Just as carefully he applied the tincture to the other foot, only this time he moved up her calf. Every stroke the tiniest of caresses. When he reached her knee, he paused and lifted his gaze to meet hers. Once again no words, but the question was there none the less.

The constant sting in her body was already lessening and a new kind of hum replacing it. A blink and smile from her was all he needed to move his fingers up over her knee. If she wasn't slowly being covered in a pasty shade of blue, she'd have sworn this was the most sensual moment anyone had ever experienced.

At the top of her knee, he stopped to gently set her foot down and she held back from begging him not to stop. Her disappointment defused slightly when he reached for her other foot and began the same gentle strokes up her calf to her knee, this time stretching the limits higher up her thigh. "You're not ticklish any more."

She shook her head. Maybe another day. Another person. But there was nothing funny about the way his fingers felt against her damaged skin. She still wasn't sure if the healing was in the cream or his touch, but as long as he didn't stop, she didn't care.

# CHAPTER FIFTEEN

Every ounce of self discipline Gil had was being strained to the limit. In his head he repeated: Pam's hurt, Pam's hurting. He reminded himself he was rendering aid, not dabbling in foreplay. Keeping himself from running his fingers up the inside of her thigh and continuing higher and higher was absolute torture. He couldn't remember the last time he wanted a woman this badly.

No, that wasn't true. He did remember. And even then, Pam had him twisted in knots battling want and desire with doing the right thing. She wasn't his anymore. "I…" He leaned back and screwed the cap onto the jar. "Angie will be back soon, she should put the rest of this on you."

Pam didn't say anything. Her eyes had gone soft, hazy. He'd like to say it was his touch that had done that to her. That the battling temptations burning inside him were ricocheting through her bloodstream as well. Just as hot and hungry as his. But he knew she was in pain, and he needed to leave.

Pushing to his feet, he sucked in a breath to clear his mind. This had been too much. Too close. "The group island tour that Kirk and the others have been planning to talk Leo into leaves the dock at 8:30. I've arranged for a cab to pick us up at 8:45. I'll swing by here and meet you."

"No." Pam shook her head. "I'll meet you at the gangway door."

Gil gave a curt bob of his head. She was right. He didn't need to come anywhere near this room again. "8:40 at the gangway. Everyone else should at least be off the ship by then. Once we're sure the tour has left, we'll meet the cab."

Even though she didn't look all that sure, Pam nodded at him.

"I'll let myself out. See you in the morning."

On the other side of the door, Gil paused to regroup. The next twenty-four hours had every sign of becoming the longest day of his life.

Pam had no idea how long she'd been staring at the ceiling when the cabin door squeaked open.

"I gather the coast is clear?"

"Of course it is." There was no point in sharing with Angie that fried to a crisp or not, she'd come within seconds of ignoring all the pain for what she knew would be immeasurable pleasure at the hands of Gil Harris.

"Are you hungry?"

Ravenous, but she was pretty sure that wasn't what Angie referred to. "A little."

"I brought a chicken Caesar salad and a milkshake." Angie set them down on the nightstand. "I figured you wouldn't want anything warm and the milkshake might help cool you down."

"Thanks."

"I've always thought you looked good in blue."

"What?" Pam followed Angie's gaze to her legs. "Oh, yeah. Feels good too. He was right. It takes the sting out."

"Why did you only put it on your legs?"

For less than half a second Pam considered filling Angie in on Gil slathering her in blue cream and burning of her skin that had nothing to do with exposure to the sun. "It hurts to bend my arms. If you wouldn't mind helping me with the rest after you eat."

"I can eat later. I cheated and drank a milkshake while I was upstairs. I ran into the anniversary couple from Peoria. We had another nice visit. They're doing the same tour as the rest of us tomorrow."

"That will be nice." The salad held little appeal at this

point, but sitting up, Pam stabbed at the leafy greens.

Blue jar in hand, Angie sat beside her. "I was out of line."

"Which time?" Pam grinned teasingly.

Angie stuck her tongue out. "What I said about all your husbands being poor imitations of your first one."

She stabbed at the salad again, staring at the way the limp leaf hung from the tines, then let the plasticware fall to the plate. "You're right. As much as I hate to admit it, my type does seem to be the same." A mature version of her prom king.

"I don't get it. When I look at the two of you, I don't see divorced couple."

Pam shrugged. "I was young, scared, and I let his mother convince me that he would be better off with someone more like him."

"And what the heck does that mean?"

"A college girl with a future." Pam blew out a long sigh. "You know, most of the town thought I was pregnant. The other half thought I'd lied about being pregnant. You might say I had a bit of a reputation before Gil and I got together. I hadn't realized how life-size it was until he left for school and I stayed behind."

"You're not the sort to let gossip bother you."

Pam shook her head. "I don't think I really cared what they said about me. It was what everyone thought about him. *That boy had to have cheese between his ears to think that girl was carrying his baby.* The one that stung hard was, *That boy will never amount to anything with the likes of her as his wife.* So when Mrs. Harris not so subtly implied I'd be holding him back and dropped hints at every opportunity that Gil was having the time of his life with his new friends. I believed her."

"Do you still think that?"

"Doesn't matter what I think now. Gil has a life that has nothing to do with me. His future is the kind of woman his mother thought he deserved."

"I have to wonder if fate isn't trying to tell you two something and you're both too deaf to hear."

"You sound like a bad fortune cookie."

Angie shook her head at her friend. "It's not my life. And Leo is a nice guy, but you've got one chance left to make this right and it runs out in less than twenty-four hours."

"Hi there." Gil stood out on deck, glad to hear Karen's voice. They'd been best friends for so long, it was hard for him not to talk to her about all the thoughts and doubts running loose in his mind. "How's everything going?"

"Do you think anyone besides my mother and father would care if I just caught the next flight to the Caribbean and skipped the big wedding?"

"That bad?"

"Not really. This just isn't…"

Gil sat in the nearest lounger and set his ankle across his knee. "Isn't what?"

"When did I lose my way?"

"What?" Gil dropped his feet to the floor and leaned forward. "What am I missing?"

"I'm sorry. There's just so many darn fires to put out with you gone, and then my mother is behaving like it's the end of the world because the caterers don't have enough of the chilled burgundy under-cloths for the extra five tables of guests she added to the list and want to substitute soft merlot."

"First, aren't those both dark reds?"

"Thank you. That's what I told Mom."

"And second, crisis management is your gift. You've put out more fires than a five alarm blaze. What's this really about?"

She took her time responding and he could picture Karen rubbing the heel of her palm across her forehead, considering her words. "Now isn't the time."

"Karen. Spit it out. I'm a big boy. What's going on?"

She sighed heavily into the phone. "Are we doing the right thing?"

Her words stopped him short. So close to her blockbuster wedding was never a good time for a bride to be asking this question. Unless of course she was suffering from a proverbial case of cold feet. Especially when the prospective groom couldn't stop thinking about the one woman he thought he'd finally forgotten. But he'd never lied to her before and he wasn't capable of starting now. "I don't know."

"So you feel it too?"

"Feel it?" Unless she had a secret husband pop up, he had no idea what she was feeling. "You lost me again."

"Something's not right. I should be more invested."

"Invested?"

"I told you I was just stressed. Maybe it's all becoming too real for me now. Not just a practical idea. Or maybe it's just you suddenly already being married coupled with my crazy mother is the universe screaming at me. Or maybe I'm over reacting to everything. Let's forget I brought it up."

"Karen—"

"No. We've planned this move for almost a year. I've just got pre-wedding jitters and the mother from hell."

"She's not that bad." He had no words for all the other bullet points. Was the universe screaming at them? Even if it was, there wasn't a blessed thing he could do about it. In two days Pam would belong to someone else.

"Let me remind you." Karen interrupted his thoughts. "Tablecloths. Chilled. Burgundy."

"Okay," he chuckled. "Maybe she's not at her best right now."

"I'd better go. I've got a few clients to call."

"I understand, but I hate leaving you so distraught." Or maybe he was the one who needed to talk this out more.

"Just call me tomorrow when it's all over. And don't worry. I'll be fine. Night."

"Night." Gil dropped his phone on the patio table and stared off at the moonlight sparkling across the dark waves. She'll be fine. Too bad he couldn't say the same thing about himself.

# CHAPTER SIXTEEN

"This shouldn't be so hard." Hands on her hips, Angie stood at the closet door. "I still say the beach tee Nancy picked up in San Juan is your best bet."

"I can't wear that to a divorce."

"There's no such thing as divorce clothes." Angie flipped her wrist. "Eight o'clock. I have to go or I won't make it off the ship on time. I'm telling you, I've seen what some of these tourists wear. No matter what you pick, you'll look fine."

"Go." Pam shooed her friend away. "Have a good time. And keep Leo busy."

Angie hesitated by the door. "Do you think you should have let him stop by this morning the way he wanted? You know, to put his mind at ease that you're resting well?"

"Does it matter?" Pam waved her arms, turning her hands palm up. "It's too late now. Everyone is on their way to the tour bus."

"Right." Angie grabbed her floppy hat. "You'll want this to protect your face from the sun."

"What about you?"

She pulled her sunglasses out of her small purse, perched them on her nose and straightened her shoulders. "I'm all set. And gone. Bye."

The door slammed shut and Pam stared at her closet. Even if she weren't burned from head to toe, literally, what *would* be appropriate divorce clothes? The cream had done wonders to help ease the sting of the burn, but she was still fried and her skin was still sensitive. Gil's t-shirt had been the perfect pajama for her. No scratchy seams. Besides, her senses memory had kicked in and his lingering scent had helped her sleep soundly. Even if her dreams had been somewhat inappropriate under the circumstances, which she could also say about the now greasy t-shirt and public appearances of any kind.

Out of options, Pam picked up the knee-length beach t-shirt that Nancy had dropped off after an early breakfast. Pink, with a design from San Juan, it fit what she needed. And Angie was right, the things some of the passengers wore onto shore was mind-boggling. Especially the two teens who seemed to think that sleeping pants was acceptable daywear. And she wasn't even going to deal with the bald headed guy in the thong Speedo. Like it or not, the pink tee-dress won.

It took her another fifteen minutes to determine none of her sandals would work and that much to her surprise her loafers were the most comfortable. With the long pink t-shirt, brown loafers, and a floppy straw hat, she looked like a cartoon criminal on the lamb, but it was what it was. At exactly eight-forty, she stepped out of the elevator and stood to the side of the small lobby area.

Five minutes later Gil joined her. "Sorry I'm late. There seems to be an excess of wheelchairs wanting off the ship as well. It took a while to get an empty elevator."

"No problem." She held her purse in her hand, her shoulder not up to the pressure of a strap.

"We should be clear to leave the ship. From the upper deck I watched the busses loading with passengers. As soon as I saw Leo climb aboard I came down."

"Okay. Let's do this."

It took a few minutes to find the right driver and settle in. Gil repeated the plan for the day to the driver.

"Where did you learn to speak Spanish?" Pam asked.

"I work with a lot of foreign investors. You'd be surprised how much money there is throughout central and south America."

"Drug money?"

"Probably, but I'm referring to the people who have always had money. The ones who own the newspapers, and factories, and other growing export businesses. Not everyone speaks English. Since high school and college Spanish wasn't going to get me anywhere, a brief immersion course made sense. It's paid for itself a hundred times over."

"I bet. Even in Bluffview, we're getting more and more immigrants. If I want to chat with the cleaning crew I'd have to speak Spanish. Which I don't." Gil nodded, and she had nothing more to add. For a brief while she got sucked into the beauty on the other side of the window. A two lane blacktop road wound through thick green foliage and towering trees.

"It's beautiful, isn't it?" It was easy to hear the smile in Gil's voice.

"It really is." She kept her gaze out the window. "A world away from Porterville."

"Do you ever wish your life had taken you somewhere else?"

She turned to face him. "All the time."

"Really?" Gil tipped his head to one side and studied her. "Where?"

"I don't know that it matters where I live." Shifting her gaze back to the countryside, she shrugged. It wasn't a *place* she missed. "I like the seasons. Though I prefer a longer summer with a shorter winter—"

"That leaves out Chicago."

Pam flung her gaze back at him. "How did you wind up in Chicago?"

"The job. Recruited out of college. It had lots of potential and it was the offer farthest away from Georgia I got."

Pam nodded. "Yeah."

Silence hung between them for a long while before Gil shifted, resting his back against the door. "What are your plans after the wedding?"

"Plans?"

"More travel plans?"

"No. I've used up all my vacation days."

"So you're going to continue to work?"

There wasn't any accusation in his tone, but the question bothered her none the less. "Of course I am. I'm good at what I do. Very good."

Gil smiled. "Settle down Red, I bet you are."

The use of his old nickname for her sent tingles shooting down her spine. "Don't call me that."

"Sorry." His smile slipped.

"No." She sighed. "I'm the one who's sorry. It's just a bit of a sore spot that I never went to college. A high school degree doesn't count for much anymore than proof that I can spell my name. College kids come in as administrative assistants and get promoted up."

"And you stay where you are."

"Don't get me wrong. I like my work and I make a good living, but sometimes I wonder…"

"What?"

"How things would have turned out if I'd been smart like you—"

"Don't say that." He sat straighter. "You knew how to appreciate all things around you. You never put people into boxes. Didn't try to fit square pegs into round holes. You hated the constraints of the classroom. Homework and tests may not have been your favorite thing, but don't sell yourself short. You were very smart. Still are. You couldn't do your job if you weren't. You know that old joke about 'who do you want to talk to, the man in charge, or the person who really knows what's going on?'"

Pam chuckled. That about summed it up. Her current boss had his act together pretty well, but the editor Kirk had replaced often made Pam wonder how he found his way to work in the morning. "Thank you."

"Just telling it the way it is."

"You do that a lot don't you?"

"I've built a career on knowing what I'm doing and shooting straight from the hip. I don't sugar coat things and I don't pretend dung doesn't stink."

"What does your mother think of Karen?" Pam didn't know why that question had popped out. Or maybe she did. Too many days were lost wondering how different things would have been if Mrs. Harris had actually liked her. Just a little support from their parents and things could have been so very different. Should have been different.

"I suppose she likes her." His expression didn't change, but Pam felt a cool shadow fall over him. "I think she's mostly hoping for more grandchildren."

"That should make her happy."

"It would if Karen wanted children."

"She doesn't?" That was odd. When she and Gil would talk about their future, Gil was the one who pictured everything with a couple of kids, usually boys, and a big sloppy dog.

"Karen is a businesswoman first. Her only baby is her dad's company. And she has big plans for it if he ever turns over the reigns."

"If?"

"Her father still sees finance as a man's world. But he's coming around."

"Does he approve of you?"

Gil laughed "You could almost say our marriage was his idea."

That made no sense. Unless. "Her father expects you to take over, doesn't he?"

"He expects a lot of things, but Karen has a mind of her own."

The road curved away from the thick trees and hugged the rocky shoreline. The view was spectacular. "I wish we had time to stop and explore."

"Maybe if the judge doesn't take too long we can stop on our way back."

She nodded her head, but somehow she didn't think walking the beach with her official ex-husband would be quite the same.

Halfway to Santo Domingo Gil and Pam had fallen into a comfortable place. It had taken a while to sift through the complications of their current situation and without an audience, settle into the rapport that had once upon a time been so natural for them. Without any further mention of Karen, or Leo, or impending weddings, or parental expectations, past or present, they managed to bring each other up to speed on the major events of their lives. He was still laughing at the day Pam discovered not only had Kirk and Michelle known each other before he'd come to work for the paper, but Michelle was pregnant with his baby.

"What a circus." He chuckled.

"Yeah, but it turned out well."

"I have to admit, it's almost sickening how happy those two are."

"I'm glad. I never really liked the back stabber she was supposed to marry."

"There's a code that good men live by. You don't poach your best friend's girl, and you certainly don't poke your best girl's friend."

"Ya llegamos." The driver announced they'd arrived as he pulled up in front of a Spanish colonial building in old Santo Domingo. By the time Gil had circled the car, the smiling man, delighted with his gringo earnings for a long day, had opened the door for Pam.

"Gracias. Donde nos encontramos?"

"Aqui, les espero."

Gil paid the man for the first leg of the journey, and ushered Pam up the sidewalk.

"What was that all about?"

"I asked where to find him later. He's going to wait for us here."

The light mood that had cloaked them for the better part of an hour seemed to dissipate with the sweltering tropical heat. Or perhaps merely with reality. The past had returned to its proper place and the present smacked them upside the head.

Inside the old building Gil felt as though he were stepping back in time. Or perhaps onto the set of some old nineteen forties film noir. Any minute he expected Burt Lancaster or Bette Davis to come strolling around the corner. A pretty young receptionist greeted them at the end of the main hall and directed them to the proper office.

The distance along the narrow hallway seemed interminable. A fevered chill crawled up his spine. Pam closed the distance between them, almost huddling beside him as they walked, and he had to assume she felt the same.

On the other side of the solid oak door, Gil had expected a courtroom of some sort, or perhaps elaborate judge's chambers. Instead he'd found a small rickety office with a low hanging ceiling fan whirring above. Behind a massive wooden desk piled high with papers and folders, a balding older man stood to greet them. "Welcome. You are here for a dissolution of matrimony?"

"Correct," Gil answered. Pam barely nodded.

"Very well. You are in agreement?"

Did this man really expect couples to travel from the States to his office if they weren't in agreement? All set to say yes, he realized Pam hadn't answered. He turned his eyes to her, surprised to see her nibbling on her lower lip.

"You are in agreement?" the man repeated.

Sucking in a breath, Pam nodded. "Yes."

"Yes," Gil echoed, not at all surprised at the hollow ache that had suddenly taken residence in his chest.

For the next few minutes, page after page of print were passed between them for signing. The knot in his stomach was painfully reminiscent of the knots twisting in his gut the first time he'd signed divorce papers. Several hardback registers followed to fill in their names, the date, and of course, more signatures.

"Very good." The man smiled. "These will be sent to the registrar. The notary will attach the proper stamps. You may retrieve the final decrees after two o'clock."

The way Pam looked at him, he knew they were both wondering why stamping a few documents as final would take so long, but they didn't have a choice and had indeed anticipated there would be a delay.

Gil extended his hand "Thank you."

"You are welcome," the judge answered politely.

It was time. The divorce was as good as done. Escorting

Pam out of chambers, Gil quickly decided he needed to call Karen. "If you can give me one second, I'd like to call home."

Pam nodded. "Of course. I'll find the ladies room and be right back."

When Pam turned the corner under the sign *Damas*, Gil pulled his phone from his pocket and hit Karen's speed dial. On the first ring she answered.

Karen must have been waiting by the phone. "It's over."

"Yes," he confirmed.

"Yes?" Surprise sounded through the phone.

"We signed the papers. The judge didn't pose any problems, not that I expected him to, and it will be final in a few hours."

"Oh. Good. But I meant the wedding."

"Ours?"

"I told my father the wedding is off."

Relief almost made him smile until a sliver of guilt pricked at his conscience. He shouldn't be pleased by her words. *Why did she do it?* "If you were worried we wouldn't be able to pull this off, you needn't—"

"No, Gil. Friends with benefits is one thing, but it's not fair to tie you to me forever. I'm married to this business and you know it."

"Karen, I—"

"Don't. Please don't try and tell me I'm wrong. You know I'm not. When I think of how if this whole invalid divorce hadn't come up..." she faded off.

They would have built the life her father wanted for her. The idea had been to follow their own plan, but going through the motions to please parents hadn't worked so well for him the first time around. "How are you doing? Telling you father must have been hard. I wish you would have at least waited for me to come home."

"Facing Dad was easier once I made up my mind. He's already working on how to turn the reception into an awards gala and a tax deduction."

"Why doesn't that surprise me?"

"Mom had to take a tranquilizer, but she'll get over it. Eventually."

"And you? You didn't answer me. How are you?"

"I'm doing better than I would have thought, which is why I'm sure I did the right thing. I'm not a young girl anymore. It's time to stop trying so hard to please Daddy."

He wasn't going to argue that point with her, but it was time Daddy noticed not only the strong woman his daughter was, but the outstanding business person as well. "Promise me you'll call if you need anything?"

"I promise, but I won't need to."

He could hear the absolute determination in her voice. Only now did he realize that the confident and secure woman he'd been friends with for so long had been slowly slipping away with every compromise and concession she'd made to appease her parents. How had he missed that?

"And Gil?"

"Yeah?"

"We both deserve more."

He didn't have to respond. Karen had hung up and Pam was on her way back up the hall. They needed to move on with the plans. Pam had a wedding to catch. To someone else. Damned if life didn't have a miserable sense of humor.

"You ready?" he asked.

Pam nodded, but didn't smile. Wasn't divorce day supposed to be happy for at least one of the two parties involved? "I guess we'd better hurry up and wait."

"Yes." Gil fell into step beside his almost officially ex-wife. Outside, he explained to the cab driver that it would be a few more hours before they could return to the ship, then he turned to Pam. "The driver suggests to kill time we go see Cathedral Primada, the Fortaleza Ozama and then walk the Calle las Damas to the palace museum."

Exhaling a heavy breath, Pam raised her fingertips to her temple and then letting her hand fall to her side, forced a smile. "I'd rather he recommend a good bar."

# CHAPTER SEVENTEEN

The last thing Pam wanted to do now was play tourist. With the technical exception of a few hours, she was about to be once again—and this time for real—a divorced woman. Relief should have been effervescing like a shaken bottle of cola, but instead she felt the same stifling ache she'd felt the first time she'd signed divorce papers and walked away from the only man she'd ever really loved.

Mid step, the shock of her own thoughts had her stumbling, only to feel the burning sensation of Gil's hand firmly clasping her arm. She wasn't simply lusting over an ancient memory. All these years and she was still in love with Gil Harris.

"Are you okay?" he eased his grip.

She bobbed her head and struggled to peel her tongue away from the roof of her mouth. "Yeah, just clumsy." He'd become everything she knew he could. He was still kind, and sweet, and funny, and easygoing, and sexy as any book cover hero. Added to that he exuded courage, strength, power. Except now, all of that, of him, belonged to someone else.

Clearly unwilling to let go of her until he was sure she was okay, he studied her from head to toe. His expression wasn't one of a man lusting after a woman, but that of someone truly concerned, even worried, about her. And didn't that make the ache in her chest rise to her throat and nearly rob her of precious oxygen. He'd been everything she wanted once upon a time, and had become everything she was looking for now. But she was part of his past, not his future.

"Isn't that the place?" Pam pointed to the nearest colorful establishment and propelled herself forward.

"That's it." Again, he fell in step beside her.

The driver who had led the way said something to the hostess, then he tipped his hat at Pam with a few words that she assumed to be a repeat of earlier in the day, then spun about and left.

"Is he waiting for us again?"

Gil smiled. "Yes. He'll come and get us when the papers are ready."

"That's nice of him."

"My guess is he's expecting an extra tip."

"Which you will of course give him."

Gil flashed a weak smile. "I will."

"This is your table," the young lady said in heavily accented English.

"Thank you." Gil slid into the u-shaped booth.

From her seat, Pam studied the surrounding area. Booths lined three walls. A few tables were scattered in the center, but most of the central area was used for a dance floor. The nearly rectangular table was clearly intended for more than just two people. Looking across the wide expanse to Gil, Pam lifted one of the menus. "I'm starved." Which was of course a bold faced lie. Her stomach had been in knots all day, but she wasn't going to let him know.

Gil opened his mouth to respond, just as the music kicked in. Though not that loud, between the distance across the table and the rhythmic beat over head, it was unlikely they'd be able to say two words to each other unless they moved to the inside of the U and sat side by side. Gil was the first to ease over. She'd made it this far, what the heck was a few more inches. Scooting her bottom along the well worn pleather seats, Pam stopped less than a foot away from her almost officially former husband. Sitting this close shouldn't affect her so much. Just a few more hours. She'd done it before, she could do it again. She hoped.

The waiter appeared, and Gil ordered a Presidente beer.

"I'll have a margarita," she requested.

"Frozen or on the rocks?" the waiter asked.

It took her a few seconds to decide, but brain freeze held an unexpected appeal at the moment. "Frozen, please."

Neither she nor Gil said a word as they reviewed the menu. Pam could have easily made up her mind if only she were able to concentrate on the print in front of her instead of the man beside her.

"I'm not really hungry." Gil set the menu down on the table.

Pam did the same. "I'm not as hungry as I thought. Just a snack would be good. Maybe they have chips and salsa?"

"That's Mexican. Closest thing I saw to chips would be the Tostones. Twice fried plantains."

Pam nodded. "The salt will go with the margarita."

Gil smiled at her and despite the churning in her gut, she smiled back at him. Maybe some day they could be friends again. Right—and rats didn't like cheese.

The waiter returned with their drinks.

"We're not very hungry. Perhaps a dish of Tostones?" Gil asked and the waiter nodded. "Do you recommend anything else for snacking?"

"Pastelitos. They're bite-sized meat filled pastries. Very good."

Gil nodded. "Some of those too please."

The first slow sip of her frozen drink went down cold and smooth. The bartender had a heavy hand. "Wow, this sucker packs a punch."

Gil chuckled and took a long pull from his icy beer. "Not bad." He bobbed his head. "Not bad at all." The server had made a big deal over the brand and serving it in a thin layer of ice. Who knew in this part of the world serving beer could be considered an art form?

Pam took another sip. And another. Already she could feel her nerves uncoiling. "Do you think the papers will be ready sooner than later?"

"Nope." Gil toyed with the corner of the bottle's label. "I don't think anything gets done fast around here."

The music switched from a local Latin rhythm to an American pop hit, the change bringing a table of tourists across the room onto the dance floor. Sipping her drink,

Pam kept her eye on one couple in particular. The only ones holding each other close, they circled the wooden floor with ease and comfort, moving as one.

"They're pretty good." Gil followed the same couple.

"They've obviously been dancing together a long time."

Gil held out his hand. "Up for a spin?"

Whether she was or wasn't didn't seem to matter, before she could consciously weigh the pros and cons of being held in Gil's arms in public view, she'd slipped her hand over his and was making her way out of the booth.

"I'll be careful of your burn."

She'd somehow managed to forget that only yesterday she'd been fried to a crisp. "It's actually much better, thanks to you and that miracle cream."

"Glad I could help." His gaze locked with hers and she almost forgot to keep moving.

Across the short distance from the table to the dance floor, Gil held onto her hand. By the time she stood circled in his arms Pam had forgotten everything that had brought them this far and let herself live in this one brief moment of how things should have been. Together they swayed and swirled as though they too had been dancing often for all these years. Gil spun her out and twirled in, and Pam actually giggled.

Gil's response was a high wattage smile that made her insides sing. The next tune was something a little faster and he let his arm fall away from her waist, but continued to hang onto her one hand. For the rest of the song they twisted and turned, neither willing to relinquish the small connection of her hand in his. Another peppy tune came on and under any other circumstances, Pam would have begged off and taken a seat to catch her breath, but this wasn't any other time. This was Gil and her last chance to just feel.

A tour bus rolled to a stop on the street outside and when the passengers moved in a single wave toward the front door, a surge of panic stiffened her spine.

"Relax, Red. That's a party bus."

The newly arrived crowd did seem a bit happy for the lunch hour.

"Those buses pick up at the local hotels and go from bar to bar."

"How do you know this?"

He grinned at her again. "I think just about every island has some Caribbean version of a party bus."

"Oh." It occurred to her that this Gil had seen more of the world than the local boy she'd married. "Do you visit the islands a lot?"

He shook his head. "My business takes me to South America more often than not. I may have managed to sneak in an island vacation or two, here or there."

Her vacations usually consisted of cleaning out closets and catching up on shopping lists. Even her honeymoons had been to nearby resorts. Except of course for her Las Vegas wedding.

The next wave of music played a soft ballad. In Spanish she had no idea what the song was, but Gil pulled her back into the fold of his arms, and without hesitation she burrowed against him. Her pulse racing, she could hear his heart echoing the same rapid rhythm as her own. Only in her case, her heart wasn't the only thing racing. Every vein throbbed with a yearning so strong, Pam almost wished the colonial hotels rented by the hour. Every fiber of her being screamed danger, trouble, beware, at the same time her heart pounded out words like, comfort, heaven, and home.

The modified two step that had taken them around the floor had slowed to a sweet, sensual sway. Unable to resist the temptation, Pam raised her head and leveled her eyes with his. The raw hunger staring back at her nearly stole her breath. "Gil," she managed to whisper seconds before his mouth cam crashing down on hers.

The tour bus pulled out of the massive parking lot and onto the road. Nancy proudly held up her hand painted platter. "I can't believe how cheap this was."

Angie had a feeling had they not been a busload of

American tourists descending en mass, the hand painted wooden plate might have been considerably cheaper still.

"Did you get anything?" Mary Jane, the wife from Peoria asked.

Angie shook her head. Trinket shopping wasn't in her budget. Nancy and Mary Jane eagerly pulled out their buys. The traditional coffee mug, a small basket. Nancy's face beamed as she held out a blue larimar and silver necklace.

"Oh that is lovely," Mary Jane cooed. "I thought about it too, but decided to wait and see what we find in Santo Domingo."

The mere mention of the capital city had goose flesh rising on both Angie's arms. She knew darn well the local courthouse was not a tourist attraction, and yet the idea of the wedding party and the soon to be divorced couple in the same city made her more than a little nervous.

The speaker system clicked from the guide's microphone. "Our next stop will be the Alcazar de Colon, or Columbus Alcazar, built by the son of Christopher Columbus, followed by lunch at a popular restaurant in Santo Domingo's Colonial Zone."

Once again, Angie forced a smile, then leaned back and closed her eyes. The stress of this week was beginning to get to her. After all, Santo Domingo wasn't a small town, they had plenty of places to eat. She was just stressing needlessly. The odds of bumping into Pam and Gil were less than slim. Still, she might just take a page from Nancy's newfound vacation strategy and drink her lunch.

# CHAPTER EIGHTEEN

There had to be a rulebook somewhere that said a man should not ravenously kiss his wife while awaiting a final divorce decree. Not that it mattered. With the weight of his impending wedding lifted, he couldn't have resisted her lips anymore now than he could back in Porterville. What he didn't know was if he should be thankful or sorry they were in a public place, and that this was as far as he could take the sizzling melding of mouths.

Pam's hand slid out from his grip to wrap both her arms around his neck, pulling him closer, deeper. Barely swaying to the slow Latin rhythms, all her soft curves hugged his firm, hard angles. If he didn't find the strength to pull away, they'd both be arrested for public indecency.

"I guess," she mumbled against his mouth, "like riding a bicycle, there are some things you never forget."

And wasn't that the truth. His senses had been on overload since the first night on the ship when she sauntered into the lounge. One by one, memory after memory had come flooding back to him, like water over a spillway. There was no stopping the feelings rushing past him. He had to letup, break away, be sensible. He may be free now, but Pam most definitely was not.

Even before Karen's call, he'd known that she deserved more from the man she married than what he could give her. And so did Pam. He only hoped that Leo loved her the way Gil had loved Pam. Had always loved Pam.

His gut tightened and sucked out what was left of the air in his lungs. *Holy divorce*. All these years and he was still in love with Pam. He smiled against her lips. "I suppose we have to stop meeting like this."

Pam stiffened in the circle of his arms. Her chest heaved with a deep breath, she kissed the edge of his mouth before taking a step back, then lifted her chin, and threw her shoulders back. He saw the reality of her plans for tomorrow pushing front and center. She might have worn a slight smile, but there was no humor in the steely eyes gazing back at him. "I don't think that's going to be a problem."

Feeling glued to the floor, Gil stood stone still, watching Pam walk toward the table where the waiter was setting their food down. His gut dropped to his shoes. Tomorrow was her wedding day to another man. How could he stand by and lose her—again.

The music picked up with another peppy Caribbean tune. The combination of guitars, percussion, and what Gil thought to be maracas drew a few more of the party bus riders across the way to their feet. Fingers snapping, hips swaying, their laughter mingled with the scratchy sound of more chairs scraping against the floor as the last of their group took to the dance floor.

A wave of smiling faces rolled past him. One of the gentlemen grabbed a girl and spun her in place. She giggled and lost her footing, shaking her head and teetered away. Less than an arm's reach away from the man left standing alone, nearly to the table, Pam had slowed her pace. Before Gil could react and catch up to her, the happy man latched onto her hand and spun her about.

Sheer horror took over Pam's face. She didn't budge. Oblivious to her lack of interest, the man shook his shoulders back and forth before grabbing hold of Pam's waist and slowly moving his feet forward and back, an exaggerated bend to his knees, he seemed to be instructing her on how to dance to the music.

Gil took a leap forward. Even if only for a couple more hours, Pam was still his wife and no one was going to manhandle her on his watch. The tiny woman who had abandoned her man a moment before must have changed her mind, because she was on a direct path to Pam and her friend, and judging by the tight press of her lips and deep crease between her brows, she was not pleased.

"Marta," a different man called, grabbing the shorter woman by the hand and twirling her into his hold. The two immediately broke into step dancing away. Whatever her mission had been a moment before was now left by the wayside.

Another couple shuffled in front of him, momentarily blocking his path. Just as he reached Pam, prepared to rescue her from the dancing stranger, the music changed again to an even faster rhythm and the entire crowd cried out, *Wopa*. The next thing he knew, Pam was spun away by yet another man, and Gil was facing a tall slender woman with swaying hips and shimmying shoulders. A quick glance in Pam's direction and his gaze locked with hers just long enough to discover not fear, or even surprise, but unadulterated humor. As if cued by a silent conductor, he and Pam burst into a fit of laughter. He could hear her thinking, *if you can't beat them join them*, as clearly as if she'd whispered it in his ear.

The Latin beats had changed from salsa to cumbia to the Dominican born merengue. Pam and Gil had held their own with the friendly group receiving lots of comments along the lines of *pretty good for an American*. One footloose couple insisted that Pam and Gil had to have Latin roots as the music played on.

Gil had considered breaking away to go eat, but burning off anticipatory energy on the dance floor was easier, and smarter, and definitely safer. Besides it gave him time to think. Their chance to step aside finally came when an Argentine Tango began to play. More cheers and roars came about as the group scattered to the edges of the floor giving space to one couple who had obviously done this before. Lean and lanky, the pair moved as one. Gil had to admit the sight was impressive, but he was ready for another beer and a little sustenance, and like it or not, he needed to talk to Pam. Really talk.

Making his way around the on-looking group, he sidled up beside the woman would be his wife for only a couple of hours longer. "I'm ready for a breather."

Pam smiled up at him, "I was ready three songs ago," then turned on her heel.

Settled again in the oversized booth, tucked together in the center, they were oddly sheltered from the crowd of partiers.

Before his lips could form a coherent sentence from the thoughts and doubts bouncing around in his head, Pam shifted her gaze from the table before them to the dancing crowd, blew out a weary breath and asked, "Did you manage to find out what the party is about?"

He bobbed his head, not sure if he was relieved or distressed by the direction of her question. "Gloria and Juan are celebrating their twenty-fifth wedding anniversary. That's the couple doing one helluva tango."

Pam's gaze drifted back to the couple surrounded by friends, hooting and cheering and applauding. "They're the same couple from a little while ago."

"Yeah." Gil followed her gaze. "The party has been ongoing for two days."

Her head whipped around. "Two days?"

"They have friends who have flown in from all over Central and South America to spend the weekend. From what I gathered, the party busses usually only run in the evening but the owner is a friend so they're starting early."

"They're going to be totally plastered by dinner." Pam fingered the fried plantain.

Gil shook his head. "Not if they spend more time dancing than drinking."

"You may be right." She nibbled on the appetizer, her eyes following the couple who had shifted from a tango to some other dance. "I don't think I realized what a musical culture Latin America is." Watching the group fill the dance floor again, Pam smiled. "These guys will probably keep dancing until the last friend boards a plane home. I think it's sort of nice."

"Dancing or the friends?"

"All of it. Being married twenty-five years and having so many friends who want to share that with you. Enough to fly from faraway ports and then spend that time laughing and dancing. It's a nice kind of happy."

"Nothing like a party back home with the women in one room and the men in another planted in front of the TV."

"Watching sports." Pam nodded.

One of the women Gil had danced with earlier slithered through the group and came up to the table. Grinning like the Cheshire cat, she reached for Gil's hand. "Come. There will be time to rest when you're dead. Now we dance. You too, Señora."

Pam held her hand up. "Thank you, but I need a little fuel." She stabbed at a pastelito she'd dropped on her plate.

Gil wondered if any part of her was searching for words to talk about what really mattered instead of polite chitchat about other couples and diverse cultures. "Give us a few minutes and we'll give it another whirl," he told the friendly woman.

Shaking her head, but still smiling merrily, the lady shrugged. "Don't forget what I told you."

Pam kept her gaze on the woman's back until she was out of earshot. "What did she tell you?"

"Not much. It was pretty loud out there." He shrugged a shoulder. "Mostly that we have one life to live."

Pam fell back against her seat, her gaze on the woman again, Pam set down her fork and nodded.

Gil wasn't going to mention the second half of the woman's comment. *"No point wasting precious time with regrets."* The pointed stare she'd aimed at him had Gil wondering if the woman somehow knew his and Pam's story. Especially when she added. *"Or second chances."*

"Boy, the place is really hopping," Michelle followed the crowd to the side room set up for the tour group. "Seems more like a disco than a restaurant."

"Even discos aren't open at noon in the states," Nancy added.

Scanning the crowd, Angie grinned. "I think it's fun."

"Pam would have loved this." Leo briefly scanned the décor.

Chairs scraped against the concrete floors, the sound mingled with clanking silverware as the busload of passengers settled in for a meal.

"I hope the food is good." George perused his menu.

Kirk did the same. "The driver says the place is popular with the locals. That's always a good sign."

"Like a truck stop," Angie added.

"Exactly." Leo set his menu aside, and sighed. "I think I'll give Pam a call and check on her."

"No!" several voices echoed nearby.

"I mean," Michelle was the first to quickly say, "You wouldn't want to disturb her if she's getting some sleep."

Nancy shrugged. "I'm sure she's fine. The one I'm more curious about is her friend. Gil."

Angie looked over at Michelle, her eyes bright with something akin to panic, and thinking fast, redirected the conversation. "Didn't the waiter say something about a Heavenly Haze? I think I'll start with that."

"Don't you usually drink diet cola?" Michelle said.

Angie shrugged. "It's been a long day. Heavenly Haze sounds heavenly."

"Good idea." Nancy nodded at Angie, then turned back to Michelle. "Think about it. Who takes a cruise to do banking business?"

*So much for redirection.*

"Investments," George corrected.

"Same thing." Nancy waved off her husband's correction. "Maybe Gil's laundering money for the mob."

"He seems so nice," Mary Jane from Peoria's face pinched. "I mean, I'm sure he's here on legal business."

"Think about it." Nancy eased forward, focusing on the only person at the table buying into her theory. "The man never actually meets with a client, but the ship stops at the Bahamas and Grand Cayman. Two excellent locations for hiding ill gotten gains."

George shook his head at this wife. "You're letting your imagination run away with you dear."

"I don't think so." Nancy leaned back in her seat.

"Maybe," Mary Jane lowered her voice, "he's with the CIA. The CIA is always doing sneaky things."

"No one said Gil was doing sneaky things." Leo shot a pointed glare at his sister-in-law.

"What about your fiancée?" Nancy asked and Angie wondered what the odds were of anyone coming out of this conversation unscathed.

Leo visibly stiffened. "What about her?"

"Don't tell me you haven't noticed those two look awfully chummy for *old friends*?"

"Most old friends are chummy." Kirk motioned for the waiter.

On behalf of her friend, Angie silently thanked Michelle's husband.

"The two words," Kirk continued, "are somewhat synonymous."

"Exactly," Leo seemed relieved to have a different perspective at the table.

"Oh for heaven's sake, Nancy. If we're going to discuss chummy, you and Gil looked pretty friendly dancing on the deck the first day." George sighed. "Let's not go stirring up trouble where there is none."

"That was recognizance. I still say investment bankers don't take two-week business cruises to the Caribbean."

"Broker," George, Kirk, and Leo echoed.

"Well," Nancy huffed.

"Maybe he's undercover with the FBI?" Mary Jane grinned, pleased with her guess.

"No," Nancy shook her head. "FBI is national. CIA is international."

"Oh," Mary Jane lit up. "What if he's one of those fancy soldiers. You know the ones who blend in anywhere and rescue people from terrorists."

This time everyone at the table turned to face Mary Jane. Even Nancy's expression reflected astonishment at the absurd suggestion that Gil was in the Special Forces.

"I think," Kirk interjected, "we should order."

"The pulled pork looks good." Michelle smiled.

Angie nodded her head. "I think I'll try that, too. And my Heavenly Haze."

"I'll try the arroz con pollo." Leo chimed in.

"Hmm. Chicken and rice. I'm in." Nancy closed her menu and looked at Leo. "And what about Gil's fiancée? Who goes on a business trip to the Caribbean and doesn't bring his fiancée?"

Angie nearly groaned out loud. This woman was worse than a dog with a bone. Somebody needed to get Nancy a drink. Preferably a double—and fast.

# CHAPTER NINETEEN

"You two still no dance?" The short lady from earlier stood at their table, shaking her head.

The music was fast paced. No need for holding Pam in his arms. No risk of getting sucked under by the whirlpool of emotions swirling inside him. "What do you say?"

The hesitation in her yes almost had him back pedaling. Who was he kidding? He was playing with fire. This entire situation had been one combustible event waiting to explode, but he couldn't help himself. Just as he was about to rescind the offer, she smiled and nodded.

"Good. Good." The woman raised her hands, applauding over head like a Spanish Flamenco dancer. "*Viva la musica.* Long live music."

The woman's antics seemed to ease the tension that had grown thick and heavy since the dancefloor kiss. With every twirl, every smile, every soft glance from her direction, Gil knew he was about to make the second biggest mistake of his life. What he didn't know any better now than before was how to avoid it.

Pam couldn't stand it any more. Her fingers encircling in his grip was driving her crazy. She wanted more than a dance. More than one last hour in some clandestine hotel. She wanted it all and damn fate for teasing her with all she'd ever wanted.

"Señor, señora." The cab driver came up beside them,

spoke to Gil and then turned away.

Gil let go of her hand. "The papers are ready."

"But it's not two o'clock?"

He shrugged a shoulder and couldn't quite manage a smile. "Just lucky I guess."

"Yeah, lucky." What little she'd eaten earlier soured in her stomach. "Do I have time to use the ladies room before we go?"

"Sure. I'll take care of the tab."

Pam nodded and scanned the area for signs.

"Over there." Gil pointed to the sign across the room underscored with an arrow that said *Damas*.

"Be right back." It took her a moment to inch back a step.

His lips tilted up in a tense smile. "I'll be here."

She took her time crossing the restaurant. Maybe if she moved slowly enough she could simply make time stop and remain in the moment—with Gil. Only there was no prolonging the inevitable. Taking her time was silly, and yet, she couldn't bring herself to hurry. Closer to the bathroom door she heard the sound of women's laughter. No surprise there. The party bus group had been laughing all through lunch.

"I can't believe she said that." The familiar voice filtered out the open door.

It couldn't be. Taking another step, Pam's heart lurched in her chest. "Michelle!"

"Pam!" her friend countered.

"Holy…" Pam slammed the bathroom door shut behind her. "What are you doing here?"

"This is where the bus brings the tourists. What are you doing here?"

"Apparently it's a hot spot with cab drivers too."

Leaning over the sink, Angie twisted around to face her friend. "Pammy," she practically sang.

*Pammy*? Pam looked from Angie back to Michelle. "What happened to her?"

"I think we underestimated the punch in the Heavenly Haze."

Angie straightened to face Pam and grinning like a loon, raised both her hands to wave hello.

A little surprised, okay a lot surprised, at seeing her dear friend more than a little tipsy, Pam looked to Michelle. "How many of those heavenly drinks has she had?"

"Three," Michelle quipped. "Angie's been keeping up with Nancy."

"Four." Angie held up five fingers.

Staring at her friend, grinning like a cartoon character, Pam didn't know where to begin. Turning to face Michelle, she waved a finger in Michelle's direction. "Why is she keeping up with Nancy?"

"Because our dear friend, your future brother-in-law's wife, has been spouting off that she thinks there's something sneaky going on with you and Gil."

"Oh hell." Pam's hand flew to her mouth.

"Well, don't get too worried." Michelle tossed a soaked paper towel into the trash and reached for a fresh one. "She also thinks Gil is in the CIA."

"What?" Surely, Pam had heard wrong. Michelle did not just say that Nancy thought Gil was in the CIA.

"Or the FBI." Michelle added.

"That," Angie hiccupped, still grinning, "was Mary Jane."

"Right." Michelle ran the clean towels under water. "Nancy's other choice was Gil is laundering money for the mob."

"Oh lord," Pam leaned against a sink. "I think I need a drink."

"Not you too," Michelle handed Angie the wet paper towel and waited for her to lean forward and set it across the back of her neck. "I can only handle so many sloshed friends at a time. At the moment, one is my limit."

"Well you won't have to handle any. Gil and I were just leaving. I gather no one has spotted us?"

Michelle shook her head and Angie looked up mumbling, "Hi Pammy," as though she'd just noticed her friend for the first time.

"I really should have stopped her at one." Michelle

rolled her eyes, helped her tipsy friend straighten, and then launched a satisfied smile in her friend's direction. "But Nancy is going to have one helluva hangover tomorrow."

"Yeah, well." Pam shook her head. "You two go back and make sure Leo and company don't look to the central dancefloor."

"Dancefloor?" Michelle asked.

"Not now. Just keep his attention elsewhere. Gil and I will make a hasty exit. You go first."

A minute later, Pam shoved Michelle and Angie out the door and waited till the count of ten to follow. She'd taken all of four steps when she heard Angie gleefully cry out, "Leeeo!"

Michelle came to screeching halt. To her left stood Pam's sort of ex-husband and to her right Pam's confused future husband.

"I was just coming to see if the ladies were okay. Angie was looking a little green around the gills," Leo explained to Gil. "I thought you were working onboard."

"Yes, well." Gil offered his disarming smile. "Turns out I needed to take care of some business here in the city."

"I see." Frowning, Leo rocked on his heels.

"Are you divorced?" Angie asked, too happily.

Gil and Leo snapped around to stare at her. Pam knew the exact moment Leo spotted her. The confusion in his gaze shifted to understanding. Not that he could possibly understand.

"What's going on?" Nancy wobbled over to Leo's side, and then spotting the crowd, her eyes widened. "Oh, hi Gil."

The massive grin spanning Nancy's face attested to Michelle's earlier comments. The woman was totally snookered.

"Hey wait for me," Mary Jane from Peoria called to her new friend, stumbling to an unexpected stop beside her. Apparently Mary Jane had also enjoyed at least a Heavenly

Haze or two.

"Are you with the CIA?" Nancy asked, still grinning.

Gil turned a painful gaze from Pam to Nancy. "Am I what?"

"The CIA?" Nancy repeated.

Silently, Gil shook his head, his gaze darting back to Pam as if answers to what was Nancy talking about were written on her face.

"The FBI?" Mary Jane added.

Again, Gil turned, this time examining the tipsy duo. "No."

"Then," Nancy spun around to face Mary Jane and waved an unbalancing arm at her "he's gotta be laundering money for the mob."

"What?" Gil's jaw dropped, forming a perfect O.

If Pam hadn't been forewarned in the ladies room, she would have been just as challenged following the absurd logic.

"He's not with the mob," Angie shook her head at the two women, teetering in place she waved a finger at him. "He's here for a divorce."

"Divorce?" Leo repeated. "You said you were engaged?"

"Come on, Ange," Michelle interrupted, grabbing hold of her friend's arm. "I think Kirk is calling you."

"Me?" Angie spun around, breaking free of the hold and almost falling over.

Leo reached out to steady Angie, and rephrased his question to Gil. "You're married?"

Angie perked up, and arm extended, spun about to point at Pam. "To her!"

"Uh oh." Michelle uttered the same words that had popped into Pam's thoughts. Only her version was less appropriate for mixed company.

This was not how she'd wanted to tell Leo. Placing a hand along his side, she nudged him forward. "I think we'd better have a seat."

"I prefer to stand." Leo didn't look angry exactly, but he didn't look pleased either.

Gil looked to Pam. She knew he wasn't going to say anything if she didn't want him to. Bless him for trying, but at this point, she had no choice. Facing her fiancé she sucked in a fortifying breath. "Leo, Gil is my first husband."

"See." Wobbly on her feet, Angie beamed.

Nancy looked momentarily perplexed. "So you're not with the CIA?"

Gil shook his head.

Pam ignored the question. "We were married straight out of high school. After he went off to college I realized quickly divorce was the best option."

"Even if it wasn't what I wanted?" Gil's voice came out almost a whisper, his tone steely, pained.

Pam shifted her attention to him, studying his eyes. They hadn't discussed what happened. What his mom had shared. Not back then. Not now. A myriad of emotions played behind those beautiful blue eyes, the one thing she was sure of—he was telling the truth. "Your mother said—"

"A lot of things."

Leo seemed to study them both with the same intensity Pam supposed he used to size up a witness. "I don't understand."

Pam blew out a breath and turned to Leo. "All these years I thought we were divorced. Turns out an incompetent clerk messed up and we're still legally married."

Leo bobbed his head. "I see."

This time, Pam was afraid he really did. "We were hoping to get a quick Dominican divorce before the wedding tomorrow. I didn't want you to find out how many times I've been married. I thought… that was best."

"Four," was all Leo added. She should have known he would know more about her than she'd shared.

"Then," Nancy whirled around on wobbly feet to face Gil, "you're not laundering money for the mob?"

"No," a chorus of voices shouted at her.

"Too bad. Never met anyone in the mob before." Nancy turned to Mary Jane. "Come on. I gotta pee."

"I think I need to sit down." Angie waddled in place.

"Yes. I think we all should." Michelle paused a

moment, when no one else made an effort to move, she linked her arm with Angie. "Come on. Let's go sit."

With only the three of them left standing, Leo looked between them. "So, now what?"

Gil kept his gaze on Pam. "The Dominican divorce is done. We were just on our way to pick up the papers. Pam is free to marry again."

"Hmm." Leo turned to Pam. "Is that the case?"

Her gaze was on Gil, she couldn't drag it away. There was so much sorrow and hope staring back at her that she had to wonder. "Your mother said you were enjoying all the parties. Making good contacts for your future."

"I was studying and practicing."

"She said a college girl would be the sort of wife that would help you in life. So did half the women in Porterville."

"I seem to have done just fine without a wife till now. And most of the women in Porterville are gossiping gnats."

"I thought being married to me would hurt you."

His gaze softened. "Not being married to you hurt me."

Leo cleared his throat. "I need to use the restroom. But just for your information, a Dominican divorce is not legal in many states, including Illinois." And without another word, he walked away.

"You heard the man." Gil took a step closer.

"You did say your attorneys would need to do an American divorce as well." She inched forward.

"I spoke with Karen. The wedding is off." Another step.

"She did?" Pam nodded, closing the gap. "That's nice."

"I can't do this again," he whispered.

At those five little words, the hope rising in her chest crashed with the force of a lead weight.

"I can't lose you. I don't care what I have to do. I need you to give me—us—a chance."

He hadn't touched her. Not a finger, only the warmth of his breath caressed her face like a gentle lover.

"I'd like that too. No," she corrected. "I *want* that too."

That was all either needed to hear. His lips slowly met hers. Unlike the heat of the earlier dance floor kiss, this tender caress held warmth, love, and the promise of many tomorrows. All of which she'd be delighted to spend standing right here, kissing Gil Harris.

His lips played with hers, easing back, his forehead dipped to rest against hers. "I love you, Mrs. Harris."

She couldn't stop the smile that pulled at the corners of her mouth. "Then I guess it's a good thing that I love you too, Mr. Harris."

# CHAPTER TWENTY – EPILOGUE

The white capped waves rolled onto the sandy beach with mesmerizing precision. The wedding package had included a ready room for the bride and the groom, separate of course, each with an open air patio and a view to die for. With the glass doors wide open, Angie could have stared at the water all day, but her place was beside her best friends for a very important event.

She didn't have any idea how Pam or Michelle did it. Although a couple of years apart from each other, both had somehow managed a cruise ship romance with chaotic consequences. Angie simply didn't have the stamina for it. All she could do was hope she'd meet her forever mate someplace more normal. Like at the office or the grocery store.

"It's almost time." Pam's gaze flickered from the digital bedside clock to her image in the mirror. Running her fingers down the strapless ivory colored ankle-length dress, it was probably the most colorless thing the woman had ever worn, she smiled with approval. Which made sense since Pam practically glowed. "I can't believe how nervous I am. I've never done this before."

Mouth's open, Angie and Michelle's heads snapped around in Pam's direction.

"You have *got* to be kidding," Michelle was the first to speak. "You've been married four times."

"Yeah, but this is my first vow renewal. This one is for keeps."

Michelle glanced from Pam to Angie and back, "Okay, I'm with you on that one. But I'm sorry, leading up to my wedding was way more nerve wracking than the actual ceremony."

"As long as you didn't take into account that you needed to get down the aisle before you threw up on someone…" Angie smiled at her former neighbor, her words trailing off.

"You would bring that up." Michelle sighed.

Pam patted her neatly coiffed hair, poked at a sprig of baby's breath, and then spinning about, looped her arm around her two best friends. "Look on the bright side. No one is throwing up now."

"Nervous or not, you look wonderful." Emily handed Pam a bouquet.

That brought a renewed grin to Pam's face. Angie had never seen her so happy. It did a girl's heart good. Maybe some day.

Nancy bobbed her head at the redhead. "I agree with my daughter. You make a beautiful bride."

"Now that we all agree, and no one is heaving their lunch, I think it's time we hit the beach." As official Matron of Honor, Michelle accepted another bouquet from Emily.

"All right." Emily grinned happily. "I'll go tell the guys we're ready."

"And I'll go take my seat." Nancy hesitated a moment. "And you really do look beautiful even if you're not marrying our Leo."

"Thank you," Pam said softly.

The last thing Angie had expected from sour puss Nancy was for her to be friendly and understanding without having a drink too many. For whatever reason, she was awfully forgiving of the situation.

"Oh, look." Standing in the open doorway, Emily pointed toward the seats set up on the beach for the ceremony. "There's Taylor and his brother."

"Oh, they came." Pam came up behind the young woman and peeked over her shoulder. They'd invited their new friends from the ship to join them, including the couple from Peoria.

"Who's that with your brother?" Michelle squinted into the distance.

All the color washed out of Nancy's face and Emily's eyes popped open wide. Something was up. "That's my son's girlfriend."

"Come on, Mom. I need to let the guys know we're ready and you need to get us a seat before they're all gone." Emily looped elbows with her mom.

Nancy's gaze darted from her son in the distance to Pam standing behind her, down to her daughter's arm tucked in the crux of her own. "I'm not going to like this am I?"

"It will be fine, Mom. I promise." Emily nudged her mother forward and smiled back at the bride before stepping off the patio onto the beach.

Gazing after the two women, Angie mumbled, "I wonder what that's all about?"

Pam sighed. "Nancy is about to find out she's a mother-in-law. Hopefully she'll be as understanding about that as she has been about Leo and me."

"Here's hoping she'll be happy about it," Michelle added.

Looking out at the pristine setting for an oceanfront wedding, Angie flashed back to yesterday and the mad dash to rearrange the plans to suit the new bride and groom. Gil insisted on doing it right. Pam and the girls had gone off in search of the perfect dress, but the really crazy part of the whole thing was that Leo had gone with Gil in search of a ring. The former groom-to-be insisted he had a jewelry connection and sure enough, in what looked like a hole in the wall set up behind an iron gate, a tiny woman unlocked the door and led them to a private room where a plump older man greeted Leo as though they'd been lifelong friends. Gil walked out the door with a rock the size of Gibraltar and a bargain price tag to match.

Later, back on the ship, she'd been walking the track on the upper deck after dinner and had been surprised to find Leo leaning on the railing watching the setting sun. When she'd come into view he'd straightened and offered a warm smile. "You doing okay?"

"I should be asking you that." Stopping beside him, she

rested her forearms on the railing. "I, uh… I'd like to apologize for earlier."

"Earlier?" Leo turned in place to face her.

"For the way I blurted out about Pam and Gil's impending divorce."

Lips pressed together, Leo's nose flared out a deep breath and then with a lift of one shoulder, he put on a resigned smile. "I saw it coming. Not the divorce part, but I saw the rekindling."

"You knew?"

"Who he was?" Leo shrugged again. "Not at first. But when I noticed the connection I looked into Gil's history a bit. My office found his previous marriage. To Pam."

"Oh."

Leo lifted his chin. "Don't look so sad. I may have deluded myself for a bit that it didn't matter, but deep down I saw it coming. I think I've been preparing myself for something like this since the first time it registered with me how Pam looked at him. Besides, I deserve someone who loves me like that again too."

If fate was just, he'd find that someone soon.

Smiling at her, the man pushed away from the rail. "We'd better get down dockside or we'll be late."

Gil had made a big fuss about everyone meeting him and Pam at the swatch of beach near the port. Angie nodded and followed Leo to the prearranged spot.

Under the moonlit night, in front of friends and all the strangers who had stopped to watch, Gil got down on bended knee. "This time I give you my word that I will do right by you. Will you marry me again Pam?"

There were a few other little soft words in there that Angie didn't hear, but the gleam in the lovebirds eyes said more than words ever would.

Pam bobbed her head steadily up and down, tears of joy streaming down her cheeks, Gil slid the ring onto her finger, and then throwing her arms around him, they shared a kiss that made just about every bystander sigh.

By morning the wedding plans had been efficiently and appropriately altered. Leo was no longer the groom but one of the groomsmen, and Kirk had graduated from guest to best man.

Now, in heels that sank in the sand giving a new meaning to a cardio workout, she made her way to the white runner. A step ahead of Michelle, she made her way to the men waiting by the minister and took her place to one side. As the minister began to speak, she looked at the couple about to renew their vows on a St. Maarten beach. Passersby would think they were here for their first wedding. Standing staring into each others eyes, holding hands, if Angie didn't know first hand how much in love they really were, she would have thought they were posing for a bridal magazine or vacation shoot of some kind. And for the first time in a very long time, this was what she wanted too. Not the crazy courtship part, but the stupid-grin-in-love part.

A few more words, a few more promises, and the happy bride and groom shared the awaited kiss. The small audience burst into cheers and applause and she watched the newly re-wedded couple almost dance down the aisle.

The music from the CD player changed. The best man and matron of honor followed the beaming couple down the makeshift aisle. Once the pair turned and walked off the white runner, Leo extended his arm. "That's our cue. Ready Angie?"

She scanned the small crowd on either side of the white runner cutting through the sand. Ready to burst with happiness for her friends, she flashed a smile that almost made her cheeks hurt, took hold of Leo's proffered arm and only a few steps behind her sort-of newly married friends, Angie raised the bouquet in front of her. "Ready."

Enjoy an excerpt from
# *Adam*


S hooting the cheating, conniving sleazebag between the eyes wasn't the best idea she'd ever had. After all, Texas was a death penalty state. On the other hand, a well-placed bullet in each ball could work. Didn't Lorena Bobbitt get off scot-free?

Margaret Colleen O'Brien glanced at the clock on the dashboard. She'd driven through the night, conjuring up the most satisfying ways to get even with Jonathan J. Cox. So far shooting his balls off was number one on her list.

Adam Farraday folded his tired body into the driver's seat of his pickup truck. Long nights like this—with no time for sleep—were an absolute killer, but, when the fates were on his side, the elation on the mornings after were beyond the best. Or, in this case, near morning. At six thirty the sun barely winked over the horizon. He had just enough time to make it back to town for a quick shower, change of clothes, another gallon of coffee and the last piece of his aunt Eileen's cinnamon crumb cake before his first appointment of the day.

*Or not.*

The car on the side of the road ahead was sleek, red, low-to-the-ground and tilting to one side. What moron drove a car like that in this lonely part of the country in the middle of the night? He could see it now: a retired balding lawyer, looking to rekindle his youth behind the wheel of a speed-trap-finding red sports car. And, if that wasn't enough, the idiot had to do it in west Texas cattle country.

So much for the shower and crumb cake. By the time Adam changed the tire for the man—who probably didn't even know where to find the spare—Adam would be lucky to get to work on time. He pulled off the two-lane road, mumbling to himself. "God, spare me from stupid city people."

Parking a few yards behind the stranded sports car, he hadn't yet had time to turn off the ignition when the fire-engine-red driver's side door opened. And an angel in white stepped out.

He blinked twice, deciding he wasn't hallucinating. The vision before him was most definitely not a balding lawyer suffering from a midlife crisis. A stunning redhead in a flowing gown stood stiffly, hanging on to the edge of the car door.

Stepping from the cab of his truck, he moved in her direction. She offered a shaky smile, and he noticed her grip on the door tightened. Standing six foot four, at the break of dawn, on a deserted backcountry highway, he could probably scare the life out of anyone, even an angel. Except this angel had no wings. She was all woman.

The closer he got, the more he could see her features. Eyes such a deep bright blue he could make out the shade even in the dim morning light. Hair cropped just above her shoulders shone with natural highlights from the sun. Another step and he saw even more clearly. His angel wasn't just a woman. She was a bride.

What was left of a veil hung slightly off-kilter, and, from the dark mascara smears on her cheeks, he didn't expect to find a groom anywhere nearby.

"Looks like you're having a little trouble."

Her brows shot up, and those bright blue eyes flashed stormy gray. "Ya think?"

He considered apologizing, though he wasn't sure what for, but opted to ignore the attitude and just deal with the car. The sooner she was on her way, the sooner he could get that shower he so desperately wanted. "Have you got a spare?"

"In the trunk."

He veered toward the front of the midengine car, while the pretty angel with the fiery tongue reached inside the vehicle for the key fob and popped the trunk. It took him all of thirty seconds to shift around the few things inside, including the one bag she had, pull out the spare, bounce it off the ground and recognize trouble. "Sorry, ma'am, but when was the last time you checked the air in this tire?"

Those same brows that shot to her hairline minutes ago curled into a sharp V; then she blew out a loud sigh. "It's not my car."

*Ookaay.* A snippy bride in a stolen car. A disabled stolen car. What a way to start what was clearly going to be a very long day. He pulled off his hat, slapped it against his thigh and drew in a long, deep breath.

"It's his," she said, her voice small. Not so fierce anymore. A glimmer of tears pooled in her eyes, seconds before she blinked them back and drew herself upright again. In control again. "A dog."

Adam let his gaze roam from the top of her head down to her toes, pausing for a brief second at her well-displayed cleavage, before settling his attention back on her face. "At least he has good taste."

The momentary flare of temper that flashed at his checking her out slid behind an expression of utter confusion. "What?"

"He has good taste in, uh, cars."

"The dog?"

"If you say so." Though his first thought was anyone who let a looker like this get away was probably an idiot too. "I can give you a ride into town, take the spare. Ned'll patch up the tire and bring you back here."

She shook her head. "I'm waiting for daylight. I have to find him."

Adam cast a quick glance around them. All he could see was miles of west Texas dirt. "Who?"

"The dog!" she snapped. "I have to find him. Or her."

*Or her?* "Ma'am, it's been a long night. I'm in desperate need of caffeine, and I have a full day ahead of me. Exactly what are you talking about?"

"The dog." She waved her arm at the surrounding landscape. "He—or she—came out of nowhere and just ran in front of me. That's when I swerved, blew a tire and wound up parked on the side of this godforsaken road. I must have hit or run over someth … Oh, God." She leaned against the car. "You don't think I hit him, do you? I mean, I'd know it, wouldn't I?"

He had no time to muster a reply, as his vision in white had pushed away from the car and darted off in search of … a dog. If someone's dog had wandered this far away from home, and she had hit him, causing her to run off the road, the animal could be curled up behind a rock, licking his wounds and slowly dying of internal injuries. Damn. The circle of life.

"Hang on," he called.

His angel in white had already hiked up her dress and flung the layers of fabric over one arm. For all the good it did her, as four-inch heels were not acceptable hiking shoes. At least the dry Texas clay was hard as rock, or the lady would be sinking with every step, like a golf tee. Her only potential risk would be breaking an ankle.

He reached for her arm to hold her still. "What kind of dog are we looking for?"

"I don't know." Her gaze scanned the area again. "Not small. Maybe medium size or a little bigger. Fluffy tail. You know, not a skinny tail like a Lab. Dark fur. At least I think so. I don't know." Tears pooled in her eyes again, and she swiped at her cheeks with her bare hand.

"You know what?" Adam pulled a handkerchief from his breast pocket and handed it to her. "Sounds to me like maybe you saw a coyote."

In an instant her tearful expression shifted to mild alarm. "A coyote?"

He bit back a smile. "They're real common in these parts, and, if that's what you saw, he's probably long gone and just fine. But …" He raised his hand to stop her from making any objections. "Just in case, you're going to sit in my truck—before you break your neck stomping around in those shoes—while I take a quick scan of the area and make sure we don't have an injured dog to deal with."

The vision in white opened her mouth, no doubt to argue, but didn't quite have enough time. Not wanting to deal with an injured dog *and* a woman with a broken ankle, Adam scooped her into his arms like a groom prepared to carry his bride over the threshold or, in this case, to deposit her in the safety of his truck.

He buried the smile that threatened to spring at her squeal of surprise—then suppressed the stream of words that came to mind as she whacked him repeatedly on the shoulder.

"Put me down!" she shouted.

"In another second."

"For God's sake, I can walk!" Legs now flailing like scissors gone mad, she hammered at him again, then pushed away and screeched loud enough for every breathing being from here to El Paso to hear. "I said, put me down!"

To prevent her from pounding on him again, he flung her over his shoulder, yanked open the truck door and, as gently as possible with 110 pounds of squirming woman, deposited her in the seat. "I'll get my bag and go look for our coyote. You stay put."

Bone tired, he was what his aunt Eileen would call dead and too dumb to fall over, but, if his misguided bride was right, and an injured dog was out there somewhere, he had to find it.

Much to his surprise, his otherwise-very-vocal bride sat in silence as he opened the back door of the quad cab, and pulled out a stethoscope.

"There!" She waved an arm and flew out of the truck. "Oh, he's limping."

"Stop." Adam stuck out his arm and grabbed her, before she ran off and broke her neck chasing after a who-knew-what. "I'll go. You stay put."

In the distance he saw a slow-moving shadow. Too big for a coyote. Damn. She was right. Somehow a dog had wound up out here in the middle of nowhere. Adam hunched down and whistled low, then called, "Here, boy."

The dog lifted his head, and, if Adam didn't know better, he'd swear the dog nodded at him, before turning and walking away.

"Oh, he's leaving!" Again she stepped forward, clearly ready to sprint after the dog. And once more he had to reach out and turn her about. "Really, miss, would you *please* let me go after him?"

She spun around in the direction of the dog. "But he's ..."

Her words trailed off, and Adam followed her glance. The dog was gone. The nearest crop of rocks for him to hide behind was too far off in the distance. No way had he made it that far in just the few seconds it had taken for them to turn around and back again. "Stay here. Please," he repeated.

Lips pressed tightly together, she nodded at him, then whispered softly, "Hurry, please."

The sun rose higher in the sky, casting a warm light across the dry Texas dirt. More than looking for the dog, Adam searched for something the dog could use for shelter. But there wasn't a blessed thing large enough to hide anything the size of the animal he'd seen moments ago. He'd reached the spot where he'd seen the dog. No paw prints. No tracks. He hadn't imagined him. They'd both seen the animal. He had to be here somewhere. Didn't he?

A few feet farther, Adam stopped to look back. He could no longer see the expression on the bride's face, but he could feel the intensity with which she watched him and the barren land around him. Probably jilted on her wedding day, definitely stranded in the middle of west Texas cattle country, yet her only concern was for an injured dog. He'd have to cut this city girl a little slack. Even if she did want to stomp about in four-inch heels and a wedding gown.

Surveying the empty land around him, Adam blew out a fast clip of short repetitive whistles and waited. Nothing. No sign of any four-legged creatures. "Okay, fellow. How did you get out here in the first place? And where the hell have you gone to now?"

# MEET CHRIS

Author of dozens of contemporary novels, including the award winning Aloha Series, Chris Keniston lives in suburban Dallas with her husband, two human children, and two canine children. Though she loves her puppies equally, she admits being especially attached to her German Shepherd rescue. After all, even dogs deserve a happily ever after.

**More on Chris and her books can be found at**
www.chriskeniston.com

Follow Chris on Facebook at ChrisKenistonAuthor
or on Twitter @ckenistonauthor

**Questions? Comments?**
I would love to hear from you.
You can reach me at chris@chriskeniston.com

www.ingramcontent.com/pod-product-compliance
Lightning Source LLC
Chambersburg PA
CBHW031417200726
48285CB00017BA/2408